Heartbreak Hills

Sharon's readers write:

"You are my favorite author. I have read the Mustang Mountain series and the Saddle Island series and I just finished the first two books in the Wild Horse Creek series!!! I am a horseback rider and it is so nice to read such wonderful books about horses!!!" —*Cassia*

"I was just wondering how many books there were in the Wild Horse Creek series. I started the first Wild Horse Creek book, *The Mystery Stallion*, a few days ago. Ever since then, I have not been able to put it down. Keep on writing!" —*Emily*

"Your books are what got me really into reading—thanks! Keep up the great work. I've wanted to get a horse for a long time, but I don't have one yet. One dog and a bunch of cats are what we have!!!" —*Your number-1-horse-craziest fan, Marian*

"Hi! I am your biggest fan. I love all your books! They're so inspiring and encouraging and just so great. I love horses. Every chance I get to ride, see, be around or do something with horses I get, I take it!!!" —*Madisyn*

*H*eartbreak *H*ills

Sharon Siamon

WALRUS
B O O K S

Walrus Books, an imprint of
Whitecap Books

PLEASE NOTE: Some places in this book
are fictitious while others are not.

Edited by Lori Burwash
Proofread by Lesley Cameron
Cover photo by Dave and Les Jacobs
Cover design by Mauve Pagé and interior
    design by Setareh Ashrafologhalai
Map by Marc Peters

Printed in Canada by Friesens

LIBRARY AND ARCHIVES CANADA
CATALOGUING IN PUBLICATION

Siamon, Sharon
    Heartbreak Hills / Sharon Siamon.

(Wild Horse Creek)
ISBN 978-1-55285-998-8

    I. Title. II. Series: Siamon, Sharon.
Wild Horse Creek.

PS8587.I225H42 2009   JC813'.54
    C2009-902689-9

The publisher acknowledges the financial
support of the Canada Council for the Arts,
the British Columbia Arts Council, and
the Government of Canada through the
Book Publishing Industry Development
Program (BPIDP). Whitecap Books also
acknowledges the financial support of the
Province of British Columbia through the
Book Publishing Tax Credit.

Canada Council   Conseil des Arts
for the Arts   du Canada

BRITISH COLUMBIA
ARTS COUNCIL

09 10 11 12 13   5 4 3 2 1

To Amy

CONTENTS

ACKNOWLEDGMENTS

Special thanks to:
    My excellent editor, Lori Burwash
    Doctor Wayne Burwash, equine veterinarian
    David and Lynn Bennett
    Taryn Boyd and Lesley Cameron at Whitecap Books
    Pat Harris and Baileys Irish Cream
    Jennifer White, Doc and Sally
    And, as always, Jeff Siamon

1
TRYOUTS

"Do your best!" Liv Winchester whispered into Cactus Jack's ear. "We've just got to make this team!" Cactus Jack, a chestnut horse with a wide, white blaze, bobbed his head as if to say he would throw his whole heart into whatever she asked.

Liv glanced to her right, where Dayna Regis chatted and laughed with the other girls waiting for the tryouts to start. No nerves for her! Dayna was sure she'd be chosen for the Rattlesnake Riders drill team. She was one of the most popular girls in town, and her horse, a palomino called Champagne, was beautiful.

There were only two spots open on the Rattlesnake Riders, Liv knew. One girl had lost her horse to colic, another had moved away. Being on the team meant you'd made it here in Rattlesnake Bend, a small Arizona town. Liv was determined to get one of those spots, even though she was a newcomer.

No one had spoken to her as she unloaded Cactus Jack from the trailer at the rodeo grounds. She hadn't been included in the fun as the other girls warmed up their horses in the ring. Now that they were standing in a row, waiting for the music to begin, she felt a familiar lump of loneliness rise in her throat.

"Where's your twin sister?" Dayna turned briefly to ask Liv. "I thought you and Sophie did everything together."

"We're not *identical* twins!" Liv bit her lip in annoyance. "We don't always like the same things. Sophie's not interested in precision riding."

"Smart girl. You two should stick to trail ridin' with those horses of your granddad's." Dayna looked down her nose at Cactus Jack. "You really think that little cow pony can make the team? I don't think so." She glanced at the line of waiting horses. "It looks better when all the horses are the same size."

"Now we've really got to make the team," Liv muttered to Cactus Jack, "if only to wipe that smug smile off Dayna's face." Cactus Jack was the best horse here, a true Spanish colonial with Arabian and Spanish Barb in his heritage. Liv could feel a flush of anger spreading across her cheeks. She thrust Dayna's insult from her mind and straightened in the saddle, picturing the complicated pattern they would ride in just another minute.

As music blared from the loudspeakers, Liv tugged her cowboy hat tight over her smooth brown hair. She leaned forward to pat Cactus Jack's neck. "This is it, fella."

Cactus Jack blew softly as if to tell her everything was going to be fine. Beside them, Champagne tossed her head and pawed the ground.

Dayna tried to soothe her mare. "It's okay, girl, take it easy now. It's the music!" she called to Liv. "Champagne doesn't like it."

Dayna *would* have an excuse, Liv thought. The truth was, Champagne wasn't nearly as well trained as Cactus Jack. Dayna's family ran a fancy guest ranch and spa called the Silver Spur, next to Liv's grandparents' spread, the Lucky Star. For generations, the two families had fought over land and water.

Liv and Sophie had never set eyes on the ranch until spring vacation this year—their father hated the desert and had discouraged visits. But the instant she saw it, Liv had fallen in love with the Lucky Star Ranch. When Gran had to go to Tucson for an operation, she was happy to stay on at the ranch with Sophie and her mom to help out. Now it looked as though they'd be here until fall. Liv had big plans for this summer, including being a member of the Rattlesnake Riders.

The music swelled. At the other end of the arena, their coach snapped the signal and shouted "Ho!" In pairs, the horses jogged into the ring. Liv and Dayna were the third pair. As the tempo sped up, the horses broke into a lope, split in the center and loped up each side of the ring.

Liv could tell Dayna was struggling to keep Champagne from bolting ahead. She was an experienced rider, but Champagne was giving her a hard time. As they met at the head of the ring to form a pair again, the mare gave a quick twist to the right. Dayna flew off her back as if shot from a rocket. She landed behind Champagne, right in the path of the next pair of horses.

Before Liv had a chance to think, Cactus Jack turned quick as lightning and began herding the oncoming horses away from Dayna's sprawled body.

There was a moment of chaos, with horses and riders going in all directions, then the coach was in the middle of the mess, giving orders, helping a dazed Dayna to her feet. "Can you go after her horse?" she barked at Liv. Champagne was galloping around the arena, looking for a way out, scattering horses in every direction.

"Let's get her, Jack!" Liv wheeled Cactus Jack around, pointing him at the fleeing mare. That was all he needed. Neatly, he cut her off in the corner, and when she tried to run in the other direction, he blocked her move. It wasn't long before Champagne knew escape was impossible and settled down. Cactus Jack moved in, calming her, letting her know she was safe.

"Good work." The coach ran up to seize Champagne's reins and motioned for Dayna to come and get her horse. Dayna, her face dirty, her walk a stiffer version of her usual hip-swinging stride, went to take over the reins.

"I'm afraid your mare needs more work before she's ready for the team." The coach shook her head, then turned to Liv and Cactus Jack. "But this fella is the real deal. He's a bit small, but we can team him with Crusty over there." She pointed to a gray Arabian on the other side of the ring. "The way he responded today he'll be a good influence on the other horses. He's in, and you, too, Liv. Congratulations."

Liv didn't dare look at Dayna. She rode back up the ring to join the other horses, her heart bursting with happiness.

The tryouts over, she walked Cactus Jack around the rodeo grounds to cool him out, then tied him to the trailer and filled his hay net. Minutes later, she saw the Lucky Star Ranch truck bumping up the dusty field.

Liv raced toward it to give her mom and Sophie the great news.

The truck backed up to the trailer hitch, and Jess Winchester stepped out of the driver's side. She was tall and slim like her twin daughters, with their same dark hair and brown eyes.

"Mom! Wait till I tell you—"

Liv faltered to a stop, frozen by the look on her mother's face.

"What's wrong?" she gasped. "Has something happened to Gran?"

BOMBSHELL

"Gran's okay . . ." Jess reached for Liv's hand.

"Then what? What's wrong?" Liv looked past her mother at Sophie, standing a few steps behind. She and Sophie couldn't hide things from each other, and she could see in her sister's pale, heart-shaped face that there was bad news. Seriously bad news.

"Let's get the trailer hitched and your horse loaded." Her mother motioned toward Cactus Jack, who was quietly munching hay. "Then we can talk."

"Why can't you tell me now?" Liv begged, but her mother shook her head, bending to adjust the trailer's tongue onto the hitch. Watching, Liv couldn't help marveling at her mother's skill. Even though Mom had left the ranch before she and Sophie were born, she remembered things like hitching up a horse trailer as if she'd never moved away.

"All set." Jess stood up, dusting off her hands. "Let's go."

They loaded Cactus Jack and Liv's riding gear inside and piled into the front seat of the pickup. Liv waited for her mother to speak, but Jess stared straight ahead as she drove out of the Rattlesnake

Bend Rodeo Grounds. She turned onto a dirt road that headed across the desert flats to the hills sheltering the Lucky Star Ranch.

Liv felt Sophie grab her hand and link their index fingers together. When they were little kids, they did that to show solidarity against anything that threatened them. What threat? Liv wondered. "Mom?" she begged. "Tell me."

"Your grandmother's fine," Jess started the conversation where she'd dropped it. But her voice was low and hoarse with strain.

Liv waited to hear the worst. "But?"

"In fact," Jess went on, "she's recovering faster than expected. And your grandfather is fed up with the city. He says he can't stand that motel any longer. He wants to come home."

"So . . . ?" Liv threw up her hands. They knew that about Granddad. He was miserable away from the ranch. This couldn't be all. Her mom was still holding something back.

Jess let out a long breath. "I had a message from my boss while you were at the tryouts. They can't hold my job open any longer."

"Oh, Mom." Liv could feel her throat constrict. She knew how important her mother's job as a head nurse in a Vancouver hospital was, especially since her parents had split last Christmas. "No more extensions?"

"No." Jess shook her head. "We have to be home by the end of next month—or else they'll replace me." She took her eyes off the road to glance at Liv. "There's more. I've been talking to your brother."

"Mark?" Liv's eyebrows rose. "What's wrong?" Her older brother had chosen to live with their father when the breakup happened. Liv missed them both, but especially Mark.

"He's failing two classes and sounds really unhappy," Jess told her.

"Why doesn't he come here?" Liv asked eagerly.

"It's too late to change schools with only two months left." Jess sighed. "And anyway, Mark isn't thrilled with the idea of the ranch."

Liv scrunched down in the seat with her arms folded. "I know. That's Dad's influence," she muttered. "But Mark would love it here—I'm sure he would."

Jess's voice took on a determined note. "I'm sorry, hon, but we have to get back as soon as we can. We're lucky Gran and Granddad can come home from Tucson earlier than we thought."

"So we're not staying for the summer?" Liv gulped. "We're not going to help Gran and Granddad run the ranch?"

"No." Her mom said firmly. "It's not what I want, but Shane will be around to help. Mom and Pop should be okay without us and you'll be back at your old school."

Liv felt Sophie squeeze her hand again. She jerked it away. How could Sophie understand? This was the end of everything.

As Liv snatched her hand away, Sophie felt the heat of her sister's anger. She knew how badly Liv wanted to stay on the ranch this summer. Glancing at her twin, she saw Liv's chin thrust in the air, her dark eyes flashing, her lips pressed fiercely together. I never want things as badly as Liv, Sophie thought. I never feel that disappointed.

She turned and stared out the window. The desert rolled past. Green creosote bushes grew in patches on the reddish brown sand. Dots of black cattle grazed far in the distance. Beyond them, fingers of hazy mountains reached for the sky. It was only the end of April, but already it was blistering hot.

They were climbing now, heading up into the hills. Sophie craned her neck to look for Shane's silver trailer. The young cowboy lived there with his dog, Tux, and his dad. Right now, Shane's father was in a rehab clinic in Tucson and Shane was spending a lot of time on the ranch. *I'll miss him.* The thought flashed into Sophie's brain. *I know I'm too young to be his girlfriend, but I'll miss him so much.*

Shane was sixteen, in high school. He seemed even older because he'd had so much responsibility from an early age. And now he'd be running the ranch with Granddad—without them.

Sophie leaned against the window, wishing the ride was over. She longed for the green lawn and tall trees of her Vancouver home, and for the sight of her quiet, sandy-haired brother. She'd have to call him—he must be miserable about failing in school. It was strange, Sophie thought, how Mark could be the same age as Shane but act so much younger.

Ten minutes later they rattled up to the Lucky Star Ranch gate. Sophie jumped out to open it, choked in the dust thrown up from the truck while it rumbled through, then shut the gate and hopped back in the cab.

Her mom and Liv hadn't said a word since Mom had dropped the bombshell about going home to Vancouver. Now, as they pulled into the ranch yard, Jess glanced Liv's way again. "You had something to tell us," she murmured. "It sounded important. What was it?"

3
NIGHT SOUNDS

"Cactus Jack and I made the Rattlesnake Riders drill team," Liv muttered as the truck rolled to a stop in front of the low barn. "As if it matters now!"

The Lucky Star Ranch had once been a showplace. Nestled in a ring of hills, surrounded by groves of live oak and *mesquite* trees, the ranch had raised prize cattle along Wild Horse Creek. But in recent years, without enough rain, the creek and wells were almost dry. The cattle were gone.

The pride of the Lucky Star was still its small herd of pure Spanish colonial horses, led by the steel blue stallion, Diego. They were the descendants of horses brought from Mexico by Maria Lopez, Sophie and Liv's great-great-great-grandmother, when the ranch was first built.

Cactus Jack was one of those horses. Sophie helped put down the ramp of the trailer and back him out. "I know how you feel," she murmured to Liv as they walked him to the barn.

Liv brought Cactus Jack to a sudden halt. "*No, you don't,*" she hissed. "For once, you have *no* idea how I feel. You've never really loved the ranch, or the desert. You've never wanted to stay."

"That's not true!" Sophie took a step back. "I love . . . some things."

"But not the way I do." Liv walked on, Cactus Jack close beside her. "This is the first time in my life I've ever known what I really want and it's all being taken away. Do you realize I beat Dayna Regis and her palomino to a place on the drill team? Not only that, but Cactus Jack saved her miserable life when Champagne threw her."

"Oh." Sophie gazed at her twin. She knew how much beating Dayna would mean to Liv. After all, just a few weeks ago, Dayna had stolen the love of Liv's life, a ranch hand named Temo who worked at Dayna's place. "But you can practice with the team until we have to go."

"No, I can't." They had reached the barn. Liv put Cactus Jack in crossties and grabbed for her grooming kit. "I'll have to tell the coach I won't be able to ride with the team. They'll have to get someone else. Poor Jack." She straightened his mane, put her forehead on his face. "All your brave work for nothing."

"But you can see that we have to go back." Sophie handed her a brush. "Mom's job . . . and Mark."

"I don't see." Liv glared at her. "Why can't you and Mom leave me here with Granddad and Gran? Why do we all have to leave?"

"Mom wouldn't go home without both of us." Sophie shook her head.

"That's the problem, isn't it?" Liv stroked the brush down Cactus Jack's side, where a white patch in the shape of a cactus was bright against his chestnut hide. "Where you go, I have to go. Just because we're twins, Mom treats us like we're one person. Why?"

"Habit, I guess." Sophie shrugged her slender shoulders. At one time, she and Liv hadn't minded the way people thought of them as a unit—the twins. But now it seemed like a coat they'd grown out of, too tight in places. She and Liv were so different.

While Liv finished grooming Cactus Jack, Sophie went to find her own horse, Cisco, a fabulous white-faced sorrel with a lighter mane and tail. He whinnied a greeting as she approached the Lucky Star herd. They were standing in the shade of the oak trees along the back of the big corral.

"Liv thinks I don't care, but you know it's not true, don't you, boy?" sighed Sophie. "You know I'll miss you like crazy, you and Shane and the ranch. I might not throw a fit the way Liv does, but I can't imagine life without you. I don't know when I might see you again, or Gran, or Shane . . ."

She rubbed Cisco's forehead in his favorite spot. "I'll have to ask Gran how old she was when she fell in love with Granddad," she whispered. "Maybe she wasn't much older than I am—almost fourteen. Granddad must have been a young cowboy like Shane."

Sophie tucked a lock of hair that had fallen in her eyes back under her hat. Unlike Liv's, her hair was fine and wild, always escaping. Like Gran's, Sophie realized. She'd been looking forward to getting to know her grandmother better. They'd only started getting acquainted when Gran had to leave the ranch for medical tests, but already Sophie felt as though Gran understood about Liv, about how hard it could be to have a gorgeous, outgoing twin, someone who always took the lead and left you trailing in the dust. Someone who won every battle you had with her.

That night, Liv couldn't sleep. She twisted and turned like a dog trying to find a comfortable spot to lie down. Each time she started to doze off, another burst of anger would shake her awake. Why couldn't her brother get along without them for just a few more months? Why did Mom cling to that job in Vancouver that she didn't even like? And why couldn't Sophie fight harder to stay on the ranch for the summer? If they presented a united front to Mom, she might let them stay . . .

Cool air wafted through the open window, bringing with it the spicy smells of the desert night. No matter how hot the day had been, the nights were always cool. A full moon, pale and silvery, shone across Liv's bed. On the other side of the room, Sophie snored softly in her bed.

Liv tossed and turned under her light blanket.

The next time she woke, it was a noise from outside that made her sit up. A muffled sound, hooves in sand. Horses, moving restlessly in the corral.

Then a horse whinnied, loud and clear. Diego! Liv tossed off her cover and ran to the window that overlooked the corral. She saw the dark shapes of horses moving in the moonlight. Was there something else moving in the shadows? A cougar or a pack of hungry coyotes stalking Diego and the other horses?

Liv strained to see, listened for more movement, but the horses had settled. She stayed at the window, watching, until the cool wind made her shiver and drove her back under the blanket. She listened hard until she fell into a restless sleep.

When Liv woke, the dawn light was streaming across the room. She was stiff from her struggle to sleep and now the gaping disaster of leaving the ranch flooded back. Sophie was still snoring. "I can't stand this!" Liv whispered.

Seconds later, she was pulling on her jeans and boots, buckling her belt and shoving her shirttail into her pants. Time to check the horses, see if there was any sign of what had spooked them last night. Might as well feed and water them, too.

She tiptoed down the narrow stairs, not wanting to wake her mom, and grabbed her wide-brimmed hat from a hook. Opening and closing the screen door carefully, Liv raced across the ranch yard, sending up little spurts of dust. She hoisted a flake of hay from the stack beside the barn and headed for the corral.

Diego and his herd had once roamed free in Wild Horse Creek Canyon, but since his battle with a mysterious black stallion when Liv and Sophie first arrived, the herd had been kept close to the ranch. It was while Liv was spreading their hay that she spotted the footprints. The horses were already milling around her, thrusting their warm noses everywhere, trampling the sand under her feet.

"Who made those big boot marks?" she asked out loud. Nobody on the ranch had feet that big, not even Shane. The prints were being scuffed out by the horses as fast as she could look for them, but over by the water trough, where the sand was damp, there was a clear set.

"Not cowboy boots," Liv said. "More like work boots with deep treads." So someone *had* been in the corral last night, and that's why

Diego whinnied. "I wish you could talk," Liv told the stallion. "But it looks like whoever it was, you scared them off. I hope it wasn't those coyotes everybody talks about!"

4

SMOKE

Everybody around Rattlesnake Bend talked about the human "coyotes." They were people who smuggled illegal immigrants across the Mexican border, along with drugs and who knew what else. Liv had seen the border patrol trucks with cages in the back for prisoners, but the smugglers had never seemed real to her before.

Now, as she stared at the boot prints in the sand, the coyotes seemed real, too real! But what would smugglers want with the Lucky Star horses? Liv shook off her fears. She'd tell Shane when he got here, and if he thought it was important, they'd have to tell Mom. She lifted her eyes to the pink-streaked sky. In the meantime, before anyone else was up, she would take a ride.

Liv knew that by noon it would be sizzling hot. The best times of the day to ride were right now and in the evening, when the sun was going down. The desert beckoned, soft and sweet in the glow of dawn. The hills to the west were touched with gold.

"Come on, Cactus Jack, we'll ride in the Heartbreak Hills. It's the perfect destination for the way I feel." She held Jack's halter up to his nose and he dipped it willingly, snorting his eagerness to be off across the desert.

As she rode away down the trail that led toward the hills, Liv gave the house a backward glance. Still no lights on. "I'll be back before you miss me," she promised the sleeping house. She had a canteen of water in her saddlebag left over from yesterday's tryouts. It was fatal to set out on a desert ride without water.

Her route led down a dusty trail through the *mesquite* and live oaks around the ranch. Liv and Cactus Jack paused to look at a small, green patch, all that was left of a shallow pond called a tank that used to hold water for the ranch stock. A few summers of drought had dried it up almost completely. No wonder Dayna's father, Sam Regis, wanted to get his hands on the spring in Wild Horse Creek Canyon. All the tanks in the region were dry like this, but the spring on the Lucky Star still flowed.

At the thought of Dayna, Liv's anger returned as harsh and burning as ever. Dayna would get that place on the drill team now! She'd gloat about Liv having to go back to Vancouver. As far as Dayna was concerned, she and Sophie never belonged on their grandparents' ranch in the first place.

"Let's go, Jack," she urged her horse, and he picked up speed as if reading her hopeless fury. They flew down the sandy trail, out of the trees and up a grassy slope. Swung around a corner of a rounded hill and out of sight of the Lucky Star.

Taking a deep breath, Liv settled into Cactus Jack's flowing stride. This was more like it—freedom, with the wild desert spaces all around. No buildings, no roads or telephone wires, no fences. Nothing but her and her horse.

Cactus Jack was everything a horse should be—swift and sure-footed, kind and intelligent. Generations of his ancestors running free in this harsh desert climate had provided the DNA for strength and stamina, good health and courage. Liv stretched forward to stroke his neck. "I love you, Jack!" she shouted. "I can't leave you!"

Half an hour later, she saw the smoke. It was just a thin trickle of gray against the light blue sky. Liv slowed Cactus Jack to take a better look. "Who would be lighting a fire out here at this time of day?" she asked aloud. Cactus Jack blew and shook his head.

Liv rode on, keeping Jack to an easy jog. Around the next corner, she came upon the campsite so suddenly that she had no time to ride out of sight. In a pocket where two hills met, the glowing embers of a small blaze sent up the plume of smoke. Around the fire were three lumps—bodies, wrapped in blankets. A large, dusty ATV was parked nearby.

Breathing quickly, Liv brought Cactus Jack to a halt. Had they heard his hooves grate on the rough sand?

One of the bundles moved, grunted. Cactus Jack, startled, let out a snort of alarm. The man under the blanket flung it off and was on his feet in a split second. Liv saw that he was wearing large work boots.

"Hey, you! What are you doing here?"

Liv didn't wait to answer. The boots and the catlike swiftness of the man's movements had been enough warning. She wheeled Cactus Jack around and sped away. These must have been the men who were at the ranch last night!

"Stop! Stop, you!"

Liv's heart pounded. She leaned into Cactus Jack's gallop. "This way!" she urged, heading him off the trail and down a steep incline.

To her horror, the ground fell away in a sandy cliff in front of them. Too late to stop. Cactus Jack plunged off the edge of the gully.

Liv felt herself flying through the air. She had no time to prepare for a landing. As her body thudded into the side of the gully, she heard a pop and felt a searing pain in her left knee.

She knew immediately what had happened. A year ago, skiing down Grouse Mountain in North Vancouver, she'd partially torn the ligaments in that knee. The tear had healed without surgery, but her knee was still weak.

This time the pain was worse. For long seconds, Liv's confused mind thought she was lying on a cold, snowy slope. When something touched her face, she reached up to grab the hand of the ski patroller who had come to rescue her. Instead, her fingers felt something ridiculously soft. When she opened her eyes, she saw Cactus Jack's long nose, sniffing her curiously.

She was in the hot, dry desert, not on a frozen ski hill. "Jack!" she gasped. "Are you okay?"

Cactus Jack blew gently. Liv raised herself on one elbow, her other arm gripping her knee. He seemed all right. "You are . . . one . . . tough horse," she gasped between waves of pain.

Her ears rang with shock, but she could hear the sound of the ATVs screaming engine somewhere above her. "Quiet, Jack," she hissed. "Stand still."

The three men must have come after her! Liv tried to reach for Cactus Jack's reins, but the pain was too severe. She knew she would black out again if she tried to stand up. Liv bit her lip so hard she tasted blood. "Please, Jack," she begged silently, "please don't move." She had rolled into the bottom of a steep gully, a twisting, narrow channel. As long as they stayed still, they were deep enough in the gully's shadow to be invisible.

The engine noise died away then increased again. Liv could hear her heart thumping to the motor's roar. The ATV was moving slowly. It stopped and her heart skipped a beat. They must not find her, not in this helpless condition.

5

DESERT VISION

"Where's your sister?" Shane Tripp's lean face creased into a grin as he came through the door of the ranch house. "Liv's usually the first one up, isn't she?" he chuckled to Sophie. "Bouncin' around here and talkin' too fast to eat." Shane had ridden in on his buckskin paint horse, Navajo, in time for an early breakfast. Tux, his black-and-white border collie, trotted at his heels.

On weekends and after school Shane helped out on the Lucky Star Ranch.

"She must have gone riding." Sophie smiled back, handing him a plate of pancakes. "Cactus Jack's not here and his tack's gone from the barn."

"Why would she do that?" Shane plunked down at the dining room table and reached for the jug of maple syrup. "She knows it's not a good idea to go out in the desert on her own."

Sophie gulped. "She's upset because we can't stay for the summer. Yesterday she made the precision drill riding team and now we have to go home as soon as Gran and Granddad get back."

"Oh," Shane said, "that's a shame." He put down the syrup. "So, you're going, too."

"We're all going . . . as soon as Gran and Granddad can come home. They won't hold Mom's job in Vancouver much longer." Sophie paused. "And my brother Mark misses us."

"How do you feel about leavin' so soon?" Shane kept his eyes on her face. "Are you . . . upset, too?" Sophie couldn't meet his gaze. Since she had made a fool of herself a couple of weeks before by letting Shane know how she felt about him, there had been an awkwardness between them. Shane thought he was too old for her, and he was right. Sixteen was just too far from thirteen, even though she'd be fourteen in September.

"I'm really sorry to leave Cisco," Sophie said. "I'll miss him like crazy. And Diego's foal, Bando—we were just starting to get the little guy used to being handled."

"I'll miss . . . all of you." Shane reached down to pat Tux, who was stationed beside his chair, waiting for something good to drop. "So will Tux, here."

Sophie came around the end of the table and knelt to ruffle Tux's silky ears. He had a black patch on one eye that made him look like a pirate. She looked up at Shane. "But we'll come back for visits— maybe next summer. I'll be almost fifteen then."

"That's a year and more from now," Shane said grimly. "Not sure I'll still be around."

The thought of Shane not being there was so bleak, Sophie had no words. She straightened at the sound of her mother's voice calling from the yard.

"I have to go to town with Mom," she told Shane. "If she asks about Liv, play it down about her morning ride. She doesn't need anything else to worry about."

Shane nodded. "I'm sure your sister'll come lopin' in any minute," he reassured Sophie. "Don't you go worryin', kid."

"I won't." Sophie smiled at him. Shane cared about her, about all of them. This ranch was really his home, and her grandparents were his family. "That's what I have to do," she lectured herself as she hurried to the kitchen. "Think of Shane Tripp as family. And someday, when I'm sixteen or seventeen, maybe he'll stop thinking of me as his kid sister."

As she hurried out the door, her mind raced forward to that happy day. Imagined his surprise when he saw how she'd changed, imagined how he'd sweep her into his arms . . .

The ATV moved on. As the motor's growl died away, Liv's racing heart slowed.

Just in time. The sun came blazing over the east side of the gully like a giant heat lamp, fixing her to the desert floor with its fierce rays. Liv hid her head in the crook of her arm. She needed water but the canteen was so high in Cactus Jack's saddlebag that it might as well have been on the moon.

She let out a hopeless groan.

All at once she felt the cool sensation of shade stealing over her. Liv squinted up. Cactus Jack had moved so that his big bulk was between her and the scorching sun.

"Good Jack," Liv sighed and shut her eyes. "You're saving my life."

An hour later, when her thirst became desperate, she tried to reach the water in the saddlebag again. The pain made her head swim. Everything went black and she fell back on the rocky ground.

Cactus Jack bent his head down to sniff her still body. Then he wheeled around and headed toward the Lucky Star.

Shane was filling the water trough with a hose when he saw Cactus Jack run in from the Heartbreak Hills to the west. The horse had his saddle and bridle on, and his reins trailed in the dust. He was breathing hard and was dark with sweat.

"Hey there!" Shane caught the reins and held him. "What's up? Where's Liv?"

He ran his hand over Cactus Jack's saddlebag. The canteen was still in it, and when he pulled it out, it sloshed. Almost full! So Liv was out there with no water. And it was getting hotter by the minute.

Shane looped the reins over Cactus Jack's neck. He let him dip his muzzle in the trough and suck up water through the bit. "Drink while you can," Shane told him. "We're gonna be on the move again in a minute."

With practiced speed, Shane saddled Navajo and set off down the trail to the west with Tux alongside and Cactus Jack on a lead rope behind. The cowboy was almost sure the horse would follow him, but he didn't want to take a chance. He might need Cactus Jack to find Liv.

Back in the hills, Shane found the cold remains of the fire and the tracks of the ATV and three men. Now he was more worried than before. There had been smugglers sighted in the area, and ranchers had been warned to watch out for any suspicious activity.

"Liv, what have you got yourself into?" Shane asked out loud, swinging back into Navajo's saddle. He had spotted the prints of Cactus Jack's small hooves leading away from the fire, running fast, and now he followed them.

Fifteen minutes later, Liv opened her eyes to find a face very close to her own. Was this a vision, or was it real? Shane had taken off his hat, and the light shone on his fair hair, his suntanned cheeks and the gold fuzz above his upper lip.

It seemed to Liv that everything she loved about the desert was summed up in that lean face close to hers. The rugged lines of the mountain ridges, the endless clear blue sky, the vivid color of the sun slanting off red rocks—it was all there in Shane's eyes and mouth and bronzed cheeks. It was the best-looking face she had ever seen.

"Liv! What's wrong?" Shane stroked her hand. His touch was cool and reassuring. Tux whimpered and licked her nose with his rough, wet tongue.

"Tux! That's enough!" Liv tried to squirm away, but the movement brought back the pain. She clutched Shane's hand. "It's my knee." She forced the words past parched lips. "I think I blew out a tendon."

"Tough luck. Don't talk. Drink." Shane held an open canteen to her lips.

Liv swallowed, coughed and gripped her knee in agony. "It hurts even when I cough. I can't move."

"Then you can't ride," said Shane. He kept his voice matter-of-fact, but they both knew this was serious trouble far from roads and people.

Liv shook her head. "Have to . . . stay still," she murmured through clenched teeth.

"All right. Lie back. I'll rig some shade and splint your leg so you're more comfortable."

Soon he had made a low sunshade using his rain gear and some long, woody agave cactus spikes. More spikes, bound with rope, held her left leg still.

Liv watched Shane while he worked. He knew what to do, no fuss or wasted effort. When he was done splinting her leg, he smoothed her hair from her face in a tender gesture, then straightened up.

"I've got to get help, but Tux here will stay with you."

"Don't leave me, please!" cried Liv. "Please, don't go."

"Won't be long. Promise."

Liv squeezed her eyes hard to keep from crying. "Leave Cactus Jack, too," she begged. "Tux is a great dog, but Jack stood over me to give me shade, and he went to find you."

Shane hesitated for a moment. "I guess you're right," he finally said. He stripped off Cactus Jack's bridle and saddle, leaving him with just his halter. "Ordinarily I wouldn't leave a horse out here on his own, but he's no ordinary horse. He'll look after you."

He swung into Navajo's saddle and rode away. The horse and the dog settled down to watch. The border collie put his black nose on his white paws, his eyes never leaving Liv's face. Cactus Jack stood patiently over her makeshift shelter, his ears pricked for any strange sounds.

6

VISITORS

"I want to get out of here." Liv glared at the nurse who brought her breakfast tray. The hospital room in Wilcox was chilly with air-conditioning. "I'm only going to be in Arizona for a little while longer, and I don't want to waste a second of it."

"I'm sure you don't." The nurse shook her head. "You can get up this morning, but I think the doctor will want to keep you for a few more days. Your knee surgery was only yesterday."

"It feels like I've been here a week already," Liv groaned.

"Well, you haven't," the nurse spoke firmly. "And you were a lucky girl to get flown in by helicopter for surgery so quickly. Your job now is to keep that leg as still as possible when you're lying down, and to get out of this bed and go for a walk."

"To the shower . . . ," Liv said hopefully.

The nurse studied her orders. "No shower until tomorrow at the earliest."

"This is horrible." Liv pulled the pillow over her head to shut out the sight of the white bed and yellow walls.

She lay there until a familiar voice asked, "Liv, are you under there?" and a slim hand pulled the pillow off her face.

"Dayna," gulped Liv, "and Temo! What are you doing here?"

"We came to see you." Dayna perched on the one chair in the small room and crossed her legs. She was wearing a white fringed jacket that set off her blonde hair. She looked, as usual, spa perfect, which wasn't surprising, Liv thought, since she lived at the Silver Spur Spa.

Temo stood behind the chair, looking down at Dayna. He was amazingly handsome, with close-cropped black hair and laughing brown eyes. Liv yanked the sheet up around her neck. I must look terrible, she thought, in this hospital gown, with my hair messed up. She hadn't seen herself in the mirror lately, but she could bet it wasn't a pretty sight.

Not that it mattered. Temo had eyes only for Dayna.

"But all the way to Wilcox?" Liv asked. "I mean, I appreciate the visit, but it's a long way to come."

"Temo drove. He had to get some special shoes for one of our horses." Dayna smiled up adoringly at him.

I get it, Liv thought. This visit was just an excuse for the two of them to be alone together. It has nothing to do with me. She sank lower in the bed, wishing they would leave.

"I felt so bad for you—making the drill team and then this!" Dayna gestured to the lumpy bandage under the blankets. "I guess you won't be ridin' for a long, long time."

"I guess not," Liv growled. Did she have to rub it in?

"But I'm sure the coach will hold your place on the team, at least for a while," Dayna went on.

Liv said, "She won't have to. We're not staying for the summer. We have to go back to Vancouver."

"You're goin' home?" Dayna's eyebrows shot up.

"Not home," Liv said. "The Lucky Star Ranch is home."

Dayna shrugged. Liv knew that Dayna thought she was pushy to even dream of belonging in her world.

"What happened out there?" Dayna drawled the question. "Did that old cow pony spook at something and toss you off?"

"Cactus Jack doesn't spook at anything!" Liv snapped back. She sat up straighter. "Since you're here"—she turned to Temo—"there's a question I want to ask you."

"Sure," Temo said kindly.

"Well," Liv began, "it's all a blur, what happened before I fell, but I think I remember some guys on an ATV chasing me and Cactus Jack."

"Up in the Heartbreak Hills?" Temo's smile faded. "Did you see their faces?"

"I . . . I can't remember." Liv struggled to straighten the tangle of memories. "I do remember they were wearing work boots, the kind with the deep treads. I wondered . . . do you think they might have been those coyotes everyone talks about?"

Temo's handsome face flushed an angry red. "I hope not. Those *hombres* give all us Mexicans a bad name. Have you told your mother about these men?"

"No." Liv shook her head firmly. "Mom has enough on her mind right now. If she thought there were smugglers in the area it would give her one more reason to leave."

"I am sorry to hear you are leaving, *muchacha*," Temo said gently.

Liv swallowed hard. Even though she knew how Temo and Dayna felt about each other, Temo had been the first guy Liv had ever had a serious crush on. And to see him head over heels about Dayna . . . Dayna, who had looked down her skinny nose at him until the day he saved her life in a cave. Then all of a sudden she realized she loved him! Her parents would have a fit if they knew.

Now, with no one but Liv to see, they stood close to each other, as if pulled by magnets. Liv couldn't stop staring at them. It was a hurt she almost needed to feel, like picking at a wound that was scabbed over.

It was a relief when she heard her mother's voice in the hall. In the next second, Sophie slipped into the room, her arms full of flowers. Jess followed and, behind her, Liv saw a face that made all the others blur.

"Shane!" His name burst out of her. It was the first time she'd seen him since he had ridden away to get help. How could she have ever thought he wasn't as good-looking as Temo? He was tall and strong, and the shy smile that tugged up one corner of his mouth made her heart race.

"The surgeon is really happy with how well you're doing." Her mother bent to kiss her, blocking Liv's view of Shane. "He figures you'll make a full recovery."

"Good." Liv peered around her mother's shoulder. "How's Cactus Jack?" she asked Shane.

"He's just fine." Shane grinned. "And you look a lot better than the last time I saw you. Does the knee feel better?"

"One hundred percent." Liv grinned back. "Of course, maybe that's the painkillers they've got me on." She smiled into Shane's blue gray eyes. He had come to the hospital to see how she was. He must really care!

"I'll get a vase for these," Sophie said. "Be right back."

Speeding down the hall with a vase provided by the nursing station, Sophie felt a strange mixture of relief and annoyance at her twin. It had been a scary day and night, but there was Liv, the center of attention, and lapping it up as usual.

It could have been worse if Shane hadn't found her so fast. If the helicopter hadn't been able to pick her up. How totally typical of Liv to go tearing off and get into trouble because she was mad about leaving the ranch, Sophie thought as she stuck flowers in the vase, filled it at the bathroom sink and carried it to the bedside table. Still, you had to say one thing for her twin sister: Liv was tough. You couldn't tell her heart was breaking to see Temo and Dayna together. Liv, who usually let the whole world know how she felt, just chattered happily to Shane.

The doctor came in. "You're a popular girl," he said with a nod.

Liv leaned forward eagerly, fixing her doctor with her vivid brown eyes. "When can I go home?"

"Maybe in a few days," he told her. "But no school for a while. I don't want you running around undoing all my careful repair on that knee. I do want you in the clinic at Rattlesnake Bend for physiotherapy treatments three times a week though. You'll be on crutches and you'll need to wear a brace on that leg."

"When can I ride?"

The doctor laughed. "If it were me, I'd never get on a horse again. But you obviously can't wait to do yourself more damage. Seriously"—his voice lost the laughter—"you won't be riding for quite a while. It's hard to say how long—but we'll monitor your recovery."

He turned to Jess. "This young lady will need some help getting around at home."

"Don't worry," Liv said. "We've got Shane to help." Now *there* was another powerful reason not to leave the Lucky Star Ranch—Shane! She felt a ridiculous grin spreading over her face and glanced quickly at Sophie. Had her sister seen how she was starting to feel about that cowboy? She and Sophie used to be able to read each other's minds. She'd have to be very careful!

SPECIAL REQUEST

"I can't get the hang of these crutches!" Liv threw them aside and sank down on the cowhide couch in the living room. Her left leg in its knee brace stuck out in front of her. She had been home from the hospital for almost a week, hobbling around the ranch. "They hurt my armpits!" she moaned to Sophie, "and it's sooo boring sitting around all day doing nothing."

"Shane's here," Sophie said. "Why don't you go and talk to him? The fresh air will do you good."

Liv gave her sister a sharp look. Had Sophie noticed how much she looked forward to Shane coming after school every day? How much time she spent leaning on the corral fence, watching him work with Cactus Jack? She loved to see the two of them, Shane sitting lightly in his western saddle, his hands and body moving in easy rhythm with the horse. They belonged here in this rugged land. And so did she.

She had asked Shane to ride Cactus Jack to keep him in condition. Despite her injury, Liv hoped for a miracle—something that would keep them in Arizona until she could ride again. Maybe not in a parade with the Rattlesnake Riders—that was too much to hope for—but just to ride her horse once more across the desert!

"Okay, I guess I'll go see what Shane's up to, if you'll hand me those stupid sticks," she said, pointing to her crutches. "I just hope he doesn't mind me hanging around all the time."

"Shane's so easygoing." Sophie smiled. "He'd never let on even if you were driving him crazy."

"Do you think I am?" Liv asked quickly. "Has he said anything?"

Sophie laughed. "It's not like you to be so sensitive. Don't worry about Shane. He can take a little attention."

But can he take two girls having a serious crush on him at the same time? Liv wondered as she hop-stepped to the door. But then, Sophie hadn't shown much interest in Shane for the past few weeks. Maybe she was getting over him. We need to talk, Liv thought, as Sophie opened the door for her.

Shane's grin as she made her way toward him on her crutches was enough to make her forget Sophie. He had fed and watered the horses in the big corral and led Cactus Jack into the smaller paddock beside the barn.

"Hi, big boy," Liv said, reaching up to stroke the chestnut's forehead. "You going for a ride with Shane? Lucky you!"

"How are you doin' today?" Shane came to stand close by her elbow. Liv felt her heart start to thump. She knew he was looking at her, so she just shrugged and kept her eyes fixed on Cactus Jack. "I'm okay," she mumbled. "Wishing *I* could ride this guy."

"The doc said it'll be awhile yet, didn't he?" Shane bent to keep Tux from tangling himself in Liv's crutches.

"Yeah, maybe a month." Liv inhaled Shane's wonderful smell of leather, horse and just plain guy. Could he hear her heart banging?

"Well, I was wonderin', since the two of us are gettin' along so good, if I could ride him in the rodeo at the beginning of June?"

Liv felt a flash of disappointed anger. "Hey! I thought you were feeling sorry for me. But all you want is my horse."

Shane frowned. "You know that's not true. I'm real sorry you can't ride. I know how much you want to, especially with havin' to go home so soon."

Liv swallowed hard. Shane understood more than he let on. She stroked Cactus Jack's smooth neck. "How do you mean ride him in the rodeo?" she asked. "Like, in an event?"

"Nah, I'm not into competition," said Shane, "but they need pick-up horses for the bareback, bronc ridin' and bull ridin' events, and they pay pretty good. I think Jack would do excellent at that. He's smart and he's quick and he don't get rattled."

Liv looked up and met his gaze. Her heart thumped harder. She frowned. "Why don't you ride Navajo? He's smart and quick, too."

Shane smoothed a saddle blanket on Cactus Jack's back. "Navajo's a good horse," he agreed, "but he'd get spooked by all the hollerin' and noise at the rodeo. I can't trust him to be steady."

"Isn't it dangerous?" Liv asked. "I mean, being in the ring with bucking broncs and mad bulls?"

"Not for a good cow horse like Jack here." Shane swung the saddle up on his back. "But if you don't want me to use him, I understand. He's special to you."

"You've got that right," Liv said. Cactus Jack had his ear swiveled toward her as though he was reading her thoughts. He was the first horse she'd cared about like he was her best friend. He picked up on her moods and feelings in a way that human friends never did. And on top of that, he'd saved her life when she'd fallen in the gully. She'd never forgive herself if he got hurt in the rodeo.

"You're sure it's safe being a pickup horse?" Liv looked searchingly into Shane's face. "Promise?"

"I promise." Shane tugged on the brim of his hat. "I wouldn't take him in the ring if I had any idea he would get hurt."

"Then I guess . . . it would be okay."

"You sure?"

Liv nodded.

"That's fine!" Shane's smile lit his eyes. He turned and started doing up the cinch. "The cash will come in handy. I can share it with you."

"You don't have to. I won't be here for the rodeo anyway. We'll be gone by then," Liv groaned. She knew how much the money would mean to Shane. With his father away in rehab, things must be tight.

"Well, thanks. But I'm real sorry you won't get to see this guy do his stuff." Shane gave Cactus Jack a pat. "All right then, fella, we'll practice some in the next few weeks. I've got lots of free time these days. Course, I'm supposed to be studying for exams, but I'd rather spend time with you."

Liv gulped. Did he just mean Cactus Jack, or did he enjoy spending time with her, too?

As he tightened the cinch, Liv studied Shane's strong profile. She was glad he needed her horse. It would give her another reason to hang around him, get him to notice her, maybe even start to like her. But first, she had to talk to Sophie, find out if she still had a crush on him.

Liv had her chance to talk to Sophie about Shane that weekend. They had been visiting the Silver Spur Ranch to train Diego's colt, Bando, every couple of days. Bando was lucky. He'd been adopted by one of Dayna's palomino mares after his mother had been killed by a mountain lion, but the colt needed to get used to being handled. After her accident, Liv just went along to watch.

"Bando's come so far in a few weeks, it's amazing." Sophie stepped in close to the colt's shoulder, keeping an eye on his front legs in case of a strike with those sharp little hooves, and on his back end in case he kicked, and on the expression in his eye that would warn her he'd had enough.

"How are things between you and Shane these days?" Liv tried to keep her voice casual, but she had to know. "You don't seem to talk to him much. Are you over him?"

"No, I'm not *over him*!" Sophie's heart-shaped face flushed. "But I try not to show it. That's one reason I'm not sorry to be going home. It's hard being around Shane and hiding my feelings all the time. Pretending I just like him like a brother."

Liv gulped. "But won't it be hard? Saying goodbye?"

"Of course!" Sophie nodded, watching the colt's expression as she stroked his cheek and fondled his mane. "But I know I'll be back some day when I'm older and more interesting to Shane."

"But what if he gets *interested* in someone else in the meantime?" Liv asked.

Sophie gave Bando a pat. "Then I'll lose him. But Shane's so steady and true, I don't think that will happen."

Liv leaned heavily on her crutches. A storm raged inside her. She couldn't betray Sophie, could she? But it was impossible to stop the rush of feelings she had whenever Shane came into a room or she heard his voice.

A smooth drawl broke into her thoughts. "Hey, Liv. How's Bando's training coming?" Dayna Regis stepped up to the corral in her white leather outfit, the fringe swinging.

"Fine," Liv answered shortly.

"I've got Champagne training for barrel racing." Dayna put one fancy boot on the fence rail and leaned close to Liv. "It was Temo's idea. He could see that she wasn't into ridin' to music." Her voice had the dreamy quality it always had when she mentioned Temo. "He's so great with animals."

Liv barely nodded. She didn't want to talk to Dayna now or hear about how perfect Temo was. She was still dealing with the bad news that Sophie had long-range plans for Shane.

"I'm pretty sure Champagne will win big money barrel racin' at the rodeo in June," Dayna went on. "Did you hear that Cheyenne took your spot on the Rattlesnake Riders? I loaned her my horse Chardonnay for the team."

"No, I didn't hear." Liv ground her teeth. Cheyenne Chase, of all people to take her place on the drill team! Fifteen-year-old Cheyenne thought she owned Shane—just because her stepmother was his aunt. She was jealous of the time he spent at the Lucky

Star Ranch and she'd be very happy they were leaving Arizona in a couple of weeks.

Dayna looked down at Liv's brace. "Must be awful borin' to be stuck out there on that dusty old Lucky Star all by yourself. When are you goin' back to school?"

"I'm not by myself—," Liv started and then caught herself. She must not talk about Shane to anyone. If Sophie ever found out how she felt! Time was running out, fast. If that miracle was going to happen, it would have to be soon. "I go back to school next week," she told Dayna.

BRADY

"Can I help you with your backpack?" A tall boy ran up the school steps beside Liv as she struggled to reach the door of the Rattlesnake Bend Junior High School late the following week.

"Sure!" Liv shrugged the heavy backpack off her shoulder so he could catch it. The crutches got in the way, and for an embarrassing moment she was face-to-face with the boy. Liv saw that he had light brown hair and bright blue eyes.

"My name's Brady Bolt, what happened to your leg?" he said in one eager breath.

"Fell off a horse," muttered Liv.

"So, you ride." Brady stayed beside Liv as she negotiated the steps on crutches. "Everybody's talkin' about the rodeo that's coming up."

"I'd be riding in it—on the drill team—if I hadn't done this." Liv made a face at her brace.

"That sucks—I mean, not the drill team, but you missin' a chance to ride in it." Brady looked flustered. "But you'll get another chance."

"Don't think so."

Brady kept pace with her as she walked to her classroom. "I'm not ridin' in the rodeo either," he explained. "My family raises bulls for the bull riding. I'd like to be a bull rider but I'm too young. Maybe next year . . ."

They had reached the door of her classroom, and Brady held it open.

"Are you in this class?" she asked. He seemed too tall to be just thirteen or fourteen.

"Never noticed me before, right?" Brady grinned. "That's okay. You're Liv Winchester, from Canada, and Sophie is your twin, right?"

"Right," Liv agreed, handing Brady her crutches and sliding into her seat with her left leg sticking out. "Can you prop these sticks somewhere for me?"

"Sure thing." Brady made off with her crutches but was back before she could get settled. "Just let me know when you need them again."

"Thanks, but Sophie sits in front of me. She'll help when I need it." Liv stared around the room at all the rodeo-themed posters and art. Brady caught her eye.

"Like I said, the rodeo's all anybody's talking about. Sure is a shame you're not ridin' on the drill team. You must have a pretty good horse."

"The best," Liv sighed, "but you'll see him. He's going to be one of the pickup horses."

"Oh, wow! Then he must be a great horse." Brady plunked down in the seat in front of her. It looked too small for him. "Do you mind if I sit here till your sister comes?"

"Be my guest." Liv shrugged.

"Thanks!" Brady perched on the chair and made a sweeping motion with his arm, sending all Liv's books flying to the floor.

"Oh! Sorry. I'm such a clumsy goof." He bent to pick them up.

"Don't worry about it." Liv smothered a laugh.

"I guess I'll go back to my own seat now," Brady said.

"Okay." Liv felt her dark mood lift as she watched him stumble back to his seat. Brady was so awkward it was funny and kind of touching at the same time.

But as the day dragged on, sitting still was torture. If one more kid tripped on her brace, made a stupid remark or stared at her like some kind of freak, she'd scream! Everybody talked about Rodeo Days, at the beginning of June. There was going to be a street dance and a pancake breakfast and a parade led by the Rattlesnake Riders. She wouldn't be part of any of it!

"Let's get out of here," she grumbled to Sophie as the bell rang at the end of the day.

Brady insisted on carrying her backpack to the truck, where their mother waited for them.

"He's nice, isn't he?" Sophie said, hopping in the cab ahead of Liv and glancing back at Brady.

"Great, if you like kids," Liv mumbled as she tossed her crutches into the back of the truck and hauled herself into the front beside Sophie. She sketched a wave at Brady as they drove off. He *was* nice, but her thoughts were too full of Shane to leave room for some eighth-grade boy, even if he was tall and not bad-looking.

As usual, Shane stayed for dinner at the Lucky Star that night. Tux perched under the table, waiting for scraps to fall or a handout from Shane.

Liv found it hard to keep her eyes off the young cowboy when he was so close. The chicken her mother had cooked was tough to swallow and the salad hard to chew. Whenever Shane was near, she would get this trembling in her stomach. She wondered if Sophie was watching Shane, too.

"The kids at school were talkin' about some smugglers up in the Heartbreak Hills," Shane said. "Temo said we should watch out for them. These coyotes are real bad dudes. I wonder if they're the same ones who made the fire I came across the day you fell off Cactus Jack and tore up your knee." He looked at Liv. "I hear they're even rustling horses across the border."

"Oh!" Liv felt a shiver of fear. She hadn't told anyone yet, not even Shane, about the noises she'd heard at night or the boot prints she'd seen in the corral. If the coyotes were looking for horses—! She quickly changed the subject, not wanting her mother to hear any more about the smugglers. "H-how did the Heartbreak Hills get their name?" she asked Shane.

He shoved back his chair. "There's a story about it," he said slowly. "Don't know if it's true."

"Tell us." Sophie shoved her hair behind her ears and settled in to listen. "I like stories."

"Well," Shane began, "there was a rivalry between two brothers who had a silver mine in those hills." He looked down at Tux. "Seems they both liked the same girl."

"Oh," Liv gulped.

"And they fought over her till the girl was scared one of them would kill the other. So she ran away and hid in the brothers' mine."

"What happened?" Sophie's brown eyes were wide.

"There was a cave-in and the girl died."

"Oh," Liv said again.

"And the brothers called it the Heartbreak Mine after that, and the hills got called Heartbreak, too." Shane ruffled the fur on Tux's neck. "End of story." He looked up. "Silly for two brothers to fight over somebody like that," he said. "It's not the strongest brother who wins—it's the one the girl picks."

Liv thought about both her and Sophie liking Shane. They were sisters—twins! Was he hinting that they shouldn't fight over him, that it was his choice in the end? That was crazy—he didn't know how she felt. Or did he?

The ring of the telephone made her jump.

"I'll get it!" Sophie cried, racing off to answer the phone on her grandfather's desk. "It's Gran!" she shouted. Their mother slid back her chair and went to the phone.

Sophie returned to the table. "I wonder why Gran's calling," she said. "I hope it's not bad news—that nothing's wrong with her."

Liv choked on a piece of chicken. The smugglers were forgotten. She didn't want to hear bad news about Gran, but it might mean they could stay longer . . . This was such a wicked thought that Liv was horrified at herself. She had wished for a miracle to keep them here but not this kind—not Gran!

"Here." Shane poured water in her glass. "Drink this. I'm sure your gran's okay."

Liv reached for the glass and their hands touched. She choked again, sure that her feelings for Shane shone on her face. "I—I have to—" She struggled to get up, to leave the table.

"Let me help." Shane was on his feet.

"NO!" Liv waved him away. "I can manage. Stop treating me like a baby!" She reached blindly for her crutches, nearly tripped over Tux and stumbled away from the table to collapse on the couch in the living room.

Her mother was still on the phone. "Give my love to Pop," she was saying, "and we'll see you on the sixteenth of June."

Jess's face as she turned to Liv was tense with worry. "They won't be able to make it until the middle of next month," she said, sinking down beside Liv.

"Is Gran okay?" Liv asked anxiously.

"She's okay, but now the doctor wants her to stay in the hospital for a few more weeks for more tests." Jess sighed. "I was hoping we'd be gone by the sixteenth."

Liv coughed to hide her gasp of relief. Her grandmother was fine and they'd be here for Rodeo Days. She'd get to see Shane ride Cactus Jack. Maybe it wasn't a miraculous solution, but it was something to look forward to.

Shane's worried face appeared in the living room door. "Everything all right?" He was looking at Liv.

"We'll be staying for another month," Jess said gloomily. "I'll have to beg them to keep my job open . . . Mark's going to be so disappointed."

Liv glanced at Shane. He was trying to hide it, but she was pretty sure he was happy they were staying longer.

"We should call Mark." Sophie picked up her cellphone as they were getting ready for bed that night. "He never says much when we talk, but I can tell he was really looking forward to us getting home. I hope he won't be too upset that we're not leaving for another month."

She paused before calling. "But I think Shane's kind of glad we have to stay," she went on. "He's so sweet."

She glanced over at her twin. Liv was sitting in front of the mirror, her leg brace stuck out awkwardly to one side. Her head was down, and her long brown hair hid her face. "Good idea," she murmured. "Call Mark."

Sophie was worried about Liv. She hadn't seemed herself lately. And she had shut Sophie out in a way she never had before. Even when they quarreled, they used to stay in touch. Now she couldn't reach Liv, couldn't tell what she was thinking.

"Is your knee hurting?" she asked softly.

"It always hurts!" Liv burst out. "What do you think?"

"You can tell me about it," Sophie went on. "You don't have to hide your feelings from me."

"I'm not hiding anything!" Liv swung around on the stool to face her. "What would I be hiding?"

"Okay, you don't have to yell." Sophie shrugged. This was an entirely new Liv, one she didn't know. Maybe she was feeling really bad about not being able to ride in the rodeo with the Rattlesnake

Riders. The rodeo was coming up, and it was all anybody at school talked about.

"Hey! I know what'll cheer you up. Let's go visit Bando again tomorrow," Sophie suggested. "It's great that we'll have another month with him before we have to leave. Maybe Shane will even come with us and give us some pointers."

As she called Mark, Sophie wondered why Liv was frowning. Maybe she didn't want Shane to help with Bando. Fine, she wouldn't ask him!

9
RODEO DAYS

Two weeks later, Sophie helped Liv climb awkwardly into the stands on the first day of the rodeo. Her crutches were gone, but she still wore a heavy brace.

"Thanks," Liv sniffed. "But I'm not totally helpless!"

"You'll soon have that brace off," Sophie soothed. "Didn't the doc say just another week?"

"Yup," Liv agreed. "Look, here come the Rattlesnake Riders."

Music blared from the loudspeakers. The riders, in their white hats and boots, sparkling blue vests and chaps, rode into the ring at a fast jog with their blue and white flags waving. Liv felt a twist of anger at the sight of those flags. She should be one of those riders, on Cactus Jack! It must feel amazing to ride to the music, keeping a steady distance between you and the next horse, thinking of the next move.

"There's Cheyenne, on Chardonnay." Sophie pointed to a rider on the far side of the third pair. As they split and rode up the sides of the ring, Liv could see that Cheyenne and her horse were half a beat behind the music. They circled and came down the center in groups of four. Cheyenne struggled to keep her horse in position.

"Cactus Jack could do so much better," Liv groaned. "If only I hadn't blown out this stupid knee." She gave her brace a smack.

The precision drill ended with a perfect pinwheel. The Rattlesnake Riders rode out of the ring to the cheers of the crowd.

Twenty minutes later, Cheyenne squinted up at them from the bench below. "I didn't know you gals were still here," she said in a loud voice. "Dayna said you were goin' back up north."

"Hey, Cheyenne." Sophie gave the short, dark-haired girl a barely polite wave.

"We're not leaving for a while." Liv shifted uncomfortably on the hard bench. "Sorry to disappoint you, Cheyenne." It was time for the saddle bronc, bareback and bull riding events. Shane and Cactus Jack would be riding into the ring. She wanted to concentrate on them.

"Doesn't matter to me if you stay or go," Cheyenne huffed. She climbed the stands to squeeze in beside Liv and Sophie. "Guess you came to see my stepcousin ride pickup in this here old rodeo."

"There's no such thing as a stepcousin!" Sophie glared at her. "Just because your stepmother is his aunt doesn't mean you're related to Shane."

Cheyenne shrugged. "Whatever . . . Look! Here he comes." She pointed at the ring. "Doesn't he look hot?"

Shane rode into the ring on Cactus Jack, his long lariat swinging. Beside him rode another cowboy on a sturdy bay quarter horse.

"GIVE THESE BOYS A BIG HAND!" the announcer shouted. "They make sure the cowboys get off the broncs and outta the ring in one piece. It takes superb riding and a superb horse to do this job. Let's hear it for our two pickup riders, Shane Tripp and Rusty Reynolds!"

Shane and Rusty raised their hats to the cheering crowd, circled the ring and then took up their positions on either side of the action.

Seconds later, the first bronc rider burst out of the chute at one end of the arena. The horse seemed to never touch the ground. It bucked, twisted, fishtailed and spun until the eight-second buzzer sounded. The crowd roared—a good ride. Shane and Rusty closed in on the still wildly bucking bronc. Shane galloped so close that the rider could cling to his waist and be swept off the bronc's back, while Rusty deftly popped the flank strap that made it buck. The bronc settled down and Rusty drove it out the gate to the catch pens.

Rider after rider repeated the performance. Most didn't last eight seconds and landed in the dust. Then Shane's job was to get the bronc away from the man in the dirt and safely out of the ring.

Liv hardly breathed through it all. Cactus Jack was so cool and quick. And Shane knew exactly what to do. After the saddle bronc event was the bareback riding, followed by the most terrifying of all rodeo events—the bull riding. The huge bulls, with their sharp horns, were bent on destroying horses, men, anything in their path. The rodeo clowns kept the maddened animals from goring the fallen riders, while Shane and Rusty tried to drive them out of the ring.

When it was over, Liv was limp with relief. With Sophie leading the way, she stumbled through the crowds to the staging area behind the ring, where steel pens held the bucking horses and the bulls.

Shane was grooming Cactus Jack in one of those pens. His grin stretched from ear to ear. "Look here!" he cried, pulling a wad of bills from his pocket to show Liv. "Enough money to last me a month!"

"You and Cactus Jack were amazing!" Sophie exclaimed. "But I was so scared for you."

Liv couldn't say anything. She hid her face in Cactus Jack's mane and stroked his sweaty side to hide her feelings.

"Hey there, he's okay." Shane's voice was right beside her.

She looked up, her heart in her throat. Shane was so adorable, so wonderful, she had to glance away again. "I . . . know." She wrapped her arms around Cactus Jack's neck to keep her shaky legs from buckling. It wasn't just the knee injury. Shane made her insides feel like they were turning to jelly.

Cheyenne had followed them down to the staging area. "Hey, cuz," she said. "Nice ridin'." Liv turned to see Cheyenne eyeing her with an expression of dawning awareness on her small face. "Guess you really love that horse, Liv, the way you're huggin' him."

Brady found Liv at the concession stand, waiting in line for a cold drink.

"Let me!" he offered. "Sit over here and I'll get you whatever you want."

"You don't have to . . . ," Liv started, but it was a relief to perch on an upturned crate while Brady stood in line, paid for the soda and rushed back to her.

"Did you see my bull?" he yelled, tripping over her outstretched leg and pouring orange drink all down his shirt. "Oh! Clumsy me. Sorry!"

"Don't worry, it's not me who's all wet." Liv shook her head, laughing, then looked up at his embarrassed face. "One of those monsters with the horns was yours?"

"Yah! The Terminator, that big red guy with the wicked horns. Nobody can ride him," Brady boasted, trying to wipe the orange stains off his shirt. "He's the meanest bull we ever raised. I bet he makes it to the National Finals Rodeo in Vegas this year."

"You sound actually proud of that creature." Liv brushed at her T-shirt, which had caught some of the orange spray.

"Sure I'm proud. Bulls like The Terminator don't come along every day. He's worth a lot of money. Do you want to see him up close?"

"I'll pass," Liv told him. "Watching those bulls from the stands was as close as I want to get."

"Someday I'm going to ride a bull like that." Brady plopped down on a crate beside her. "Then maybe you'll look at me the way you look at Shane Tripp."

Liv fanned herself with her hat. *Was it as obvious as that?*

"It's so obvious." Cheyenne tipped up her small chin. "Liv is madly in love with Shane."

"What are you talking about?" Sophie stared at her. They were high in the stands, watching the barrel racing. Dayna and Champagne were up next.

"Anybody can see it!" Cheyenne gave her a sideways glance. "She looks at him like he's some kind of rodeo star."

"You're crazy!" Sophie shouted over the bellow of the loud-speaker.

Cheyenne shrugged. "And all this time I thought it was you who had a crush on my cousin. You're both way too young for him, you know that."

Dayna was waiting in the alley. The announcer had called her name.

Sophie's head whirled. This is Cheyenne, she reminded herself. You can't trust her. Out loud she said, "Stop calling Shane your cousin. Of course we're too young. But what makes you think that Liv . . ."

The explosion of action below brought the conversation to a stop.

"Go, Dayna!" roared Cheyenne. Dayna galloped Champagne around the first barrel, then the second, dashed for the third at the end of the arena, spun around it with a horsehair to spare and rode like the wind for the alley.

Cheyenne was standing and cheering. She collapsed beside Sophie. "Great ride," she gasped. "Her time will be the best yet."

As they waited for Dayna's time to be announced, Sophie gripped the edge of the bench.

"What makes you think Liv likes Shane?" she repeated.

"Are you blind?" Cheyenne gave her a pitying look. "Just watch her the next time they're together. You'll see what I mean."

She was up on her feet and cheering again as Dayna's time was announced. Sixteen point five seconds. It put her in the lead. Sophie hardly heard. Her mind was spinning through scenes of Liv and Shane since Liv's accident. They'd spent so much time together. But Liv would never do that to her!

10

THE TERMINATOR

That night Liv limped up to Shane as he was cleaning his saddle in the barn. She gazed at him with shining eyes. "Cactus Jack was magnificent today," she said. "And so were you."

"Magnificent is a pretty big word for some plain ridin'." Shane rubbed polish into the pommel. "But thanks for lendin' him to me. Tomorrow should be a good day, too. You comin'?"

"As if I'd miss it." Liv laughed. "But I was petrified when those bulls were in the ring."

"Don't worry. I won't let them near Cactus Jack."

"I know. I trust you." Liv took a step closer. There was a question she'd been wanting to ask him since her accident. "Shane, when you came to rescue me the day I fell . . . ," she began.

"It was Cactus Jack you want to thank for that." He took another scoop of saddle soap from the can.

"I know, but did you see anyone else out there in the Heartbreak Hills?"

"No, just the fire and some tracks." Shane turned to look at her.

"There were three guys on an ATV." Liv gulped, hating to relive the moment. "They . . . saw me and I think they chased me. That's why I rode Jack over the edge of the gully." She hesitated. "Temo thought they might be those coyotes, those smugglers everybody talks about."

"Maybe." Shane polished hard with his cloth. "You know that mine I was tellin' you about—the Heartbreak?"

Liv nodded.

"The mine and the old town are on government land. Hardly anybody goes up there anymore, the road's all washed out. But I've heard that the coyotes hide out in the ghost town. Don't know if it's true. The border police can't seem to find them—course that's why they call them coyotes, 'cause just like those varmints, they can disappear like a puff of smoke through a narrow crack. Hard to catch."

He stopped polishing his saddle and turned to look at Liv again. "Did you tell your mother about the guys who chased you?"

"N-no," Liv stammered. "Because I wasn't sure they really were chasing me, or if I just panicked. And Mom has enough to worry about." She took a deep breath. "But what I really wondered was why they'd be snooping around the ranch."

"Around here?" Shane rubbed his chin in surprise. "You saw them at the Lucky Star?"

"I'm not sure about that either." Liv hurried to tell him everything. "The night before my accident, I heard Diego whinny, and the next morning I saw footprints in the corral. Big work boots like one of the guys was wearing." She paused. "Do you think they might be after the horses?"

Shane hoisted his saddle up onto the tack room rack. "Could be. Have you heard or seen anything like that since then?"

"No." Liv shook back her thick dark hair.

"If you do, tell your mom, or me. If they were the coyotes, they wouldn't be happy you'd spotted them." Shane put his arm around Liv's shoulders. "You were lucky."

"Lucky you came along," Liv burst out. She was glad Shane hadn't laughed at her fears. Glad he was around to protect all of them.

"Well, I got to be gettin' home. See you in the morning—at the rodeo," he said.

"Yeah, see you." They were standing close together. Liv heaved a big sigh. "There aren't going to be many more mornings when I'll be able to say that. Gran and Granddad will be home in a couple of weeks—and then we have to go."

"I'm sorry about that." Shane's voice was low and full of regret. "Real sorry."

Outside the tack room, Sophie fell back against the stalls, every limb of her body shaking. It was true! She couldn't mistake the look in Liv's eyes, or Shane's arm draped around her shoulders, or the regret in his voice that she was leaving.

Shane and Liv! They mustn't find her here. She crouched down out of the light that spilled from the tack room, crept out of the barn and ran to the far side of the corral, where the horses were milling close to the fence. Sophie slipped through the bars of the fence and found Cisco in the fading light.

She wrapped her arms around her horse and sobbed into his long mane. He was the only one she could turn to. "I can't believe it," she whispered. "Liv knows how I feel about Shane. How could she?"

Cisco turned his head and blew in her ear, as if to comfort her. "But maybe it isn't Liv's fault," Sophie cried in anguish. "Maybe Shane led her on. Maybe he really likes her!"

Cisco snorted.

"What should I do?" Sophie pleaded. "Oh, Cisco, what am I going to do?"

The second day of Rodeo Days was fiercely hot. The thermometer outside the barn was practically red to the top by the time they loaded Cactus Jack in the trailer and drove to the fairgrounds. Music blared from the carnival rides, and the air was sticky with the smell of spun candy and doughnuts as Liv and Sophie walked to the rodeo ring.

"I wish Shane and Cactus Jack weren't in the ring for the bull riding," Liv groaned to Sophie. "The bulls look so wicked—like they'd like to kill everything in sight."

Sophie said nothing. What was wrong with her, Liv wondered as they climbed the stands. Sophie didn't speak until they had reached their seats above the chutes.

"I can't believe it," she said in a low, furious voice, "and you know why, Liv? Because I trusted you. I never dreamed you'd go behind my back like that with Shane."

"What are you talking about? What makes you think . . . ?" Liv stared at her twin. Sophie's cheeks were scarlet.

"Cheyenne!" Sophie shouted. "She told me I was blind about the two of you, but I couldn't believe it till I saw it with my own eyes."

"Cheyenne, that troublemaking snake!" Liv bit her lip. "She just wants Shane to herself."

"But she's right, isn't she?" Sophie demanded. "You *do* like him. You've been flirting with him behind my back."

"I haven't . . ." Liv shoved down her hat. "Okay, if you want the truth, I like Shane, a lot."

Sophie's face went white. Her angry words ran together, spilling out before she could stop them. "When we first met him, you said he wasn't your type. But I know what happened. You got bored after you hurt your leg—or you decided Shane was better than nothing—since Dayna had Temo!"

"That's not true!" Liv wiped the sweat off her forehead.

"Maybe not. Maybe you worship him like some kind of hero since he rescued you." Sophie was glaring at her, her eyes full of tears.

"It's not just hero worship," Liv protested, but there was enough truth in Sophie's words to make her squirm.

"Has he kissed you?" Sophie demanded.

"No." Liv's eyebrows shot up. "I suppose he's kissed you?"

Sophie was trembling from head to foot. "You're not even sorry, are you?" She threw back her shoulders. "I'm glad we're going home. I hate this place—I hate you!"

She turned and thumped down the stands. Liv watched her race away, running as though wild bulls were chasing her across the rodeo grounds.

"I couldn't go after her if I wanted to, with this brace," Liv whispered to herself. "And even if I wanted to, I couldn't help the way

I feel about Shane." She saw him ride into the ring on Cactus Jack, totally at ease. "Look after each other today," she begged them quietly. The bucking horses twisted and squirmed in their narrow chutes, waiting for their turns to burst into the ring with riders on their backs. Sophie's scorching words rang in Liv's ears.

The bronc riding and bareback events passed and the sand was raked for the bull riding. Bulls replaced horses in the chutes. Shane and Cactus Jack stood to one side of the ring, ready for the action.

Brady, flushed with excitement, raced up the stands with another cold drink and a bag of popcorn in his hands. "Everybody's talkin' about The Terminator!" He plopped down beside her. "All the bull riders want a crack at him."

"Why, if he throws everybody off?" Liv brushed away the popcorn that had landed in her lap.

"Don't you know anything about bull ridin'?" asked Brady. "They all want the baddest bull because if they can ride him, they'll get the highest score and win big money." He sucked back his soda. "But nobody can ride The Terminator."

"How do they decide who gets to ride him?" Liv gazed at the huge animal in the chute below her. The red bull radiated enormous power, stamping, snorting, kicking in rage at the bars that held him prisoner.

"They draw names," Brady explained. "That little guy in the helmet, Jesse Sanders, drew The Terminator today. He won't last three seconds, you watch!"

"But he might get hurt," protested Liv. "Your bull might even kill him. Doesn't that bother you?"

"Part of the game." Brady shrugged. "Guys get busted up, but hardly anybody gets killed."

Liv shook her head. She'd never understand bull riding, she decided. Right now she just wanted it to be over, and Cactus Jack and Shane to be out of danger. She watched one rider after another get thrown, tossed, hurled into the air like rag dolls by the furious animals.

The last bull was The Terminator. Liv slid forward on her seat. She saw Jesse settle on The Terminator's back and wedge one gloved fist around the handhold. Other cowboys tried to hold the bull in the chute. Jesse signaled, the chute banged open and the red bull exploded out.

The Terminator's fifteen hundred pounds of muscle rose into the air like a balloon filled with the hot air of outraged dignity. When he came down, he twisted and corkscrewed. A moment later, Jesse's limp body hurtled off his back straight into the path of the bull's sharp horns.

The rodeo clowns moved in like lightning. They bobbed, danced and waved at the bull, trying to draw his attention away from the rider. The Terminator lowered his head and charged. But the clowns were faster and scrambled up the arena fence and over, out of danger. Jesse stumbled out of the ring before the bull had a chance to turn for another attack.

This left The Terminator alone in the ring with just the pickup horses to catch the full force of his fury. Shane rode at him, trying to turn the bull toward the open gate at the end of the arena.

Instead, the bull turned and faced Cactus Jack. Here was something to charge.

Liv covered her eyes. She couldn't watch. There was a loud clang and a roar from the crowd. She peeled one hand away to see the bull running down the alley to his pen, while Cactus Jack circled the ring to loud applause.

Weak with relief, Liv watched Shane raise his hat to the crowd. He had kept his promise, Liv thought. The danger was over. Cactus Jack had not been hurt.

Liv suddenly wanted Sophie there to squeeze her hand and share this moment. Instead, Brady clutched her arm. "Did you see that?" he crowed, spilling more popcorn in Liv's lap. "The Terminator tossed him off like a pesky fly. *Nobody* can ride that bull."

Liv stood up, brushing the kernels off her jeans. Leaving Brady still cheering and jumping for joy, she limped down the stands and went to find her horse and Shane. She saw them from a distance. Shane was leading Cactus Jack through the maze of pens behind the arena to the horse trailer.

To her right and left were the heavily barred pens holding the bulls. There was The Terminator, terrifying close up, so massive his dark red body seemed to fill the entire pen. Liv paused to stare at him, and at that second, there was a loud crash as The Terminator lunged at the gate. It swung open. Liv heard shouts and screams as people scattered, but she was frozen to the spot in the narrow alley, her leg brace like an anchor. The bull wheeled and faced her. Liv saw everything in slow motion—the bull's deadly sharp horns, his furious red eyes, the drool pouring from his mouth, the dust rising as it pawed the ground between them.

He lowered his head and took a step toward her. Liv heard shouts and warnings as if they were coming from far away. "Move!" "Climb the fence!" "Get out of there!" But she couldn't move.

And then she heard the pounding of a horse's hooves racing toward them. Cactus Jack! He let out a loud, ringing neigh, challenging the bull to turn and face him.

The bull shook his head from side to side, the froth at the corners of his mouth flying. With an agility and speed Liv wouldn't have believed possible for such a huge animal, he spun around to face the horse with a bellow of rage.

Cactus Jack kept coming. Liv watched in horror as the bull's deadly horn tore across his flank. Jack's quickness saved him as he dodged out of the way of another thrust. Frustrated, the bull rampaged down the alley. Two more horses went down. There was a wild scuffle as people and horses fled from his path. Liv saw cowboys struggling to rope the bull and drag him away.

Liv threw herself forward. "Jack! Are you all right?" she sobbed. Blood was pouring from his wound, soaking her clothes and knee brace.

In the next second, Shane was running toward them, his fear and guilt plain on his face. "I tried to hold him, but he saw what was happening. He yanked the reins out of my hand!" Shane gathered Cactus Jack's dragging reins. "Somebody get the vet!"

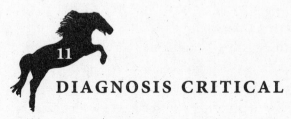

11

DIAGNOSIS CRITICAL

Two days later, Sophie hesitated outside the Lucky Star barn. Mom had sent her to get Liv for school.

Finally, she took a deep breath and opened the barn door. It was still cool in the early morning, and shafts of sun filtered through dust in the air. Low voices came from the back of the barn. That would be Shane and Liv, Sophie thought bitterly. Since Cactus Jack's accident, Liv had spent every minute in the barn. All of that time, Shane was with her.

A low whicker drove her forward. Whatever she felt, the horse was more important. The vet had told them the next twenty-four hours were critical.

"That you, Sophie?" Shane called. "Any word from the vet when he'll get out here?"

Sophie heard the worry in his voice. At the rodeo, the vet, Dr. Ruffman, had stopped the bleeding and treated Cactus Jack for shock. He couldn't say definitely whether the horse would live or, if he did, be able to run again. Meanwhile the wound was contaminated, and there was always the risk of infection or colic after such a severe trauma. Dr. Ruffman was treating him with an antibiotic.

"Yeah, it's me." Sophie walked forward. "No word from the vet. Mom sent me for Liv." She paused, taking in the scene in the large box stall. Cactus Jack was on his feet, but his head hung low. The dressing on his flank hid the fearful wound torn by the bull's horn. Tux lay in the straw, watching him.

Sophie's mouth went dry. "Mom says you have to go to school today," she croaked to Liv. "She says come to breakfast."

Liv shook her head. Her dark hair was a tangled mess and her face was streaked with tears. She had replaced the blood-soaked brace with a smaller one—her knee was getting better and in her worry over Cactus Jack she barely noticed the pain. "I'm not leaving him," she said.

"Mom told me to tell you to come, too, Shane." Sophie turned to him. Shane without his hat looked younger. His fair hair was plastered flat, and the lines around his mouth and eyes were tight with worry.

"I figure to stay," was all he said.

"I'm sure Cactus Jack doesn't need both of you in there." Sophie was looking only at Shane.

"Liv can go," said Shane.

"He's my horse." Liv's voice was low.

"And it's my fault that he got hurt," Shane muttered. "I shouldn't have asked you to let me ride him in the rodeo."

"My fault, too." Liv stared up at Shane. "If I hadn't gone riding off like an idiot in the first place—if I hadn't torn my knee, you wouldn't have been riding him in the rodeo." She reached out to stroke Cactus Jack's cheek. "This is all my fault."

"Don't cry, Liv." Shane put his hand on her shoulder.

Sophie had seen enough. "I'll tell Mom neither of you wants to eat or go to school then," she said in a trembling voice.

"Sophie?" Shane looked up at her. "I know this is hard on you, too. You hate to see animals suffer."

"That's not the only thing that's hard!" Sophie said it before she could slam the jealous words back in her mouth.

"What are you talkin' about?" Shane took a stride toward her, his face full of concern. "Is it because you have to leave? Did your mom get more bad news from home?"

"N-no." Sophie turned away. She couldn't talk to Shane about Liv. Not now, not when her traitor twin was standing right there. Maybe not ever.

"I don't understand why you aren't talking to each other." Jess glanced at her daughters at the dinner table that night. "Aren't things bad enough with Cactus Jack hurt that you don't need to make them worse? I've never seen the two of you like this."

"Don't want to talk about it," Liv mumbled. She was gobbling her meal so she could get back out to the barn with Shane and Cactus Jack.

"I realize you're worried about Cactus Jack and nobody is happy about going back to Vancouver . . . ," Jess began.

"*She* is." Liv pointed her fork at Sophie.

Their mother ignored her. "And somehow this has all become my fault," she went on. "But have either of you stopped to think about how I feel?"

Liv put down her fork and looked up. To her amazement, their mother's eyes were filled with tears.

"If I didn't need my job, and if it weren't for Mark, I'd be happy to stay here for a long time. I'm not sure I ever want to go back to Vancouver—or any big city. I was just starting to remember how much I love the desert, how much I missed this ranch." She waved around the cozy room. "And now I'm pulled away."

Liv stared. She *hadn't* thought about her mother's feelings—hadn't dreamed she shared her own.

"So, Liv and Sophie, if you wouldn't mind trying a little harder to get along"—Jess put a weary hand to her head—"you'd make things easier for me. Sophie is just trying to be supportive. I'm sure she doesn't want to go any more than you do, Liv."

Liv shoved back her chair and stood up, leaning on the table for support. "She said she hates it here, didn't you, Sophie?"

Sophie flushed an angry red. "And you know why!"

"All right, that's enough!" Jess slammed her hand down on the table. "Sophie, help me clean up. Liv, if you insist on sleeping in the barn, get Shane to help you make a proper bed."

Sophie's face was scarlet. She started to speak, but Jess held up her hand.

"Think about what I've said. We have some tough days ahead of us. We'll get through them better if you two aren't at each other's throats!"

Liv waited until Sophie had vanished through the kitchen door before going upstairs. She brushed her teeth and hair and changed her clothes. Grabbing a blanket and pillow from her bed, she vowed she'd never spend another night sharing a bedroom with Sophie.

Maybe she'd move downstairs to Gran's bedroom once Cactus Jack was out of danger or . . . Liv didn't let herself think of the alternative!

The barn light burned low. "Go and get something to eat," she told Shane as she entered the stall.

"Not hungry," he murmured.

Liv thought he'd lost weight in the past couple of days. His eyes were dull, and there were deep shadows under them from exhaustion. "Go on," she urged. "I'll come and get you if there's any change."

"Why doesn't Sophie take a shift?" Shane asked. "Then you could get some sleep." He looked down at her, his hat tipped to one side. "Your sister's actin' kinda funny," he said. "Any idea what's wrong?"

Liv gave him a shy smile. "I guess she's jealous that you're spending so much time with me."

She watched disappointment and anger cloud Shane's lean face. "So that's it! You darn kids. I wish you'd both just GROW UP!" he stormed out of the stall, Cactus Jack's water bucket swinging.

With growing anxiety, Liv watched while Shane worked silently, filling the bucket, taking extra care as he checked the dressing on Cactus Jack's flank and administered the antibiotic injection. He didn't look at Liv the whole time.

"I'll be goin' then," he said finally. "I won't stay the night." He held Jack's head between his lean, strong hands and rested his head on the horse's forehead. Tux sat at attention, his eyes on Shane's face. "You have a good night, old boy," Shane whispered. "I'll be back tomorrow."

Liv heard his boots pound away. Fear swept over her. What had she done? She should never have let him know how she and Sophie were feeling! In her despair, she turned to Cactus Jack. He had been her source of strength and solace through all this past stormy month.

"Jack, I'm sorry I drove Shane away," she murmured. "Please, *please* get better."

Sophie came in an hour later, while Liv was rubbing Cactus Jack down and trying to get him to drink. "How is he?" she asked, biting off the words.

"The same."

"Where's Shane?"

"He went home."

Liv didn't look at her. She was glad Sophie couldn't see her face clearly as she bent over Cactus Jack's bucket.

"What did you say to him?" Sophie demanded.

"Nothing."

"I don't believe you." Sophie's voice was cold.

12

ONE TOUGH HORSE

"Mom says you *have* to go to school this morning." Liv looked exhausted, with tangled hair and filthy barn clothes. Sophie wanted to tell her how sorry she was about Cactus Jack, but the words stuck in her throat. She was still too angry about Shane.

"What about my horse?" Liv stroked his cheek.

"She says the vet is coming at nine and she wants to talk to him anyway."

Liv felt a chill. Would they be discussing whether to put Cactus Jack down? "I'm not leaving him," she insisted. "I want to be here when the vet arrives." She patted Jack's shoulder. "You have to drink and eat more before he comes," she whispered.

She looked at Sophie. "Is Shane having breakfast?"

"He didn't come for breakfast." Sophie turned to go. "I still think you must have said something to make him stay away. He feels so guilty about Cactus Jack—he wouldn't leave unless he had a good reason."

Liv had no answer. She buried her head in Cactus Jack's mane. "Just tell Mom I'm not going to school," she muttered. "I don't care what she says."

The time dragged until Dr. Ruffman arrived. He didn't speak as he examined Cactus Jack from nose to tail, changed the dressing on his flank and gave him another injection. He came out of the stall wiping his hands, but with no expression on his young face.

Liv wondered how he could show so little emotion. Didn't he know how much his next words would mean to her?

"I can't find any structural damage," he said at last to Jess. "The wound is healing, although it will probably leave him with a scar. His fever is down and the infection seems to be responding to the antibiotic. At this point I expect him to make a full recovery, but there's always the unexpected . . ." He turned to Liv. "The most important thing now is to get him eating and drinking normally. You can take him out of the stall and walk him around the paddock when it's cooler. A couple of days should make a big difference."

"Then he'll be able to run again, and everything?" Liv felt a burst of joy.

"These Spanish colonial horses are tough." The vet gazed at Cactus Jack in admiration. "I've heard stories of them carrying a rider for hours when they were badly wounded and still surviving. He's got a lot of spirit, this guy. I think he'll be fine."

Liv limped back through the stall door and threw her arms around Jack's neck. "Did you hear that?" she whispered in his ear. "You are one tough horse! Eat and drink and walk and you'll get better." She turned to beg her mother, "Please, Mom, can I stay with him one more day?"

"All right." Jess gave a defeated sigh. "You'll be leaving that school soon anyway, and I don't think you'd get any work done even if I made you go." She held out her hand to the vet. "Thanks, Doc. If you come to the house, we'll see about your bill."

Liv waited all that long, hot day to tell Shane the good news. Maybe when he found out that her horse was going to get better, he'd stop being so mad at her.

It was evening—after she'd walked Cactus Jack around the paddock—when they finally heard from Shane, and then it was just a phone call.

Liv stood in the office, leaning on her granddad's desk. "Dr. Ruffman said the damage is mostly superficial," she answered Shane's question. "I'm supposed to walk him outside, but Mom says I have to go to school tomorrow. You can? That's good. Okay, see you."

She put down the phone.

Sophie appeared in the doorway. "What did he say?"

Liv sighed. "He said he has a study day tomorrow and he'll come out and look after Cactus Jack while we're at school."

"He's not coming for dinner?"

"No."

"Or breakfast tomorrow?"

"No." Liv stared at her sister. "He said he'll be here around nine— after we catch the bus."

"I wish you had let me talk to him." Sophie glared at her.

"He didn't ask." Liv brushed past her sister. What, she wondered, had she done to make everybody so mad at her? What was so awful?

Just because she was only thirteen didn't mean her feelings weren't real. Didn't mean she couldn't fall in love with someone!

ON THE BUS

The Rattlesnake Bend school bus picked up both junior high and high school students from the isolated ranches in the area. Dayna and Temo were already on it when it stopped at the Lucky Star gate the next morning. Sophie knew at once something was wrong. Temo sat in the back of the bus, his face flushed and angry-looking. Dayna was near the middle, and she had obviously been crying. Her mascara had made two black smudges on her cheeks and her eyes were red.

Temo called, "How is Cactus Jack?"

"Better," Liv called back. She slipped into a seat near the front of the bus.

Dayna patted the seat beside her and Sophie slid into it. "What's wrong?" Sophie whispered.

"Temo and his family are talking about leaving the ranch," Dayna said in a low voice. "Going back to Mexico."

"For how long?" Sophie gasped.

"I don't know." Dayna grabbed Sophie's wrist. "They're trying to help Temo's cousin get his visa to come live here. I'll—I don't know what I'll do if Temo leaves." She shook her shoulders as if to shake off that thought. "When do you two go home? It must be hard for Liv to leave poor old Cactus Jack hurt so bad."

"We're not going for a week or two—he'll be better by then," Sophie said.

"I hope he is." Dayna leaned closer to Sophie. "Don't tell your sister about Temo. She might spread it around and I wasn't supposed to tell anyone."

"Don't worry," Sophie muttered. "I won't tell."

The next stop was Shane's travel trailer. It sat alone on a flat stretch of desert, except for a pile of hay and a small run-in shed for Navajo. The bus driver pulled up, honked the horn and cranked open the bus door.

A blast of dry desert air rolled in. "Where is that boy?" the driver grumbled.

Liv and Sophie were silent. It wasn't anyone's business if Shane was out at their ranch.

The driver waited a few more minutes. Then she closed the door and the bus rumbled on its way.

At the final stop, on the outskirts of Rattlesnake Bend, Brady and Cheyenne got on the bus along with half a dozen other kids. Sophie saw Brady head straight for Liv and plop down on the seat opposite her. Cheyenne paused at the front, scanning the passengers, then raised an eyebrow at Liv. "Feelin' lost without Shane ridin' on the bus with you, Liv?" she asked in her clear, piercing voice.

"Why would I feel lost?" Liv glared at the dark-haired girl.

"Come on! Everybody at the rodeo could see you're crazy about him." Cheyenne grinned at the eager audience of bus riders.

Sophie watched everybody staring at Liv's scarlet face. She felt her own cheeks turn pink. Liv broadcasts her feelings so clearly you might as well put them up on a giant movie screen, she thought miserably.

As the day dragged on, Liv heard whispering and giggles spread around her like a brush fire.

"Is it true?" Brady was the only one to ask, peering at Liv with a mixture of sympathy and disappointment as they headed to the cafeteria for lunch. "Never mind. I've seen the way you look at Shane—like he's some kind of superhero."

"I—I'm sorry . . ." Liv tried to think of something else to say.

"Sure. None of my business anyway." Brady took off down the steps with his awkward loping stride.

Liv avoided Sophie during lunch. She took her sandwich and drink outside in the blazing heat and sat on a bench to eat. Even there, the sly glances and comments behind hands continued. She and Sophie were the talk of the school. We never really fit in here, Liv thought, and now they have a reason to laugh at us.

It was a relief to see that Cheyenne wasn't on the bus as they climbed aboard after school. She must have Rattlesnake Rider practice, Liv thought. As they passed Shane's trailer on the way home, she saw that Navajo's corral was empty. Shane might still be at the Lucky Star when they got home! Liv hoped he wouldn't hear the gossip that had swirled around school that day.

As the bus stopped in a cloud of dust at the Lucky Star gate, Sophie brushed past her, hopped over the gate and took off at a run for the house.

Liv headed for the barn. The door was slightly open. Her feet made no sound as she started for Cactus Jack's stall. Shane was with him.

Liv bent to ruffle Tux's coat. For a minute, no words would come, and then she stammered, "H-how is he?"

"Comin' along," Shane muttered without looking at her. "I gave him his antibiotic, so he's set for tonight." He smoothed Cactus Jack's side. "I should get home now and study for my science exam, but I can come back and look after him tomorrow night."

"Okay," Liv said wearily. "Bye, Tux." She bent over the dog again so her feelings wouldn't show. Tux jumped up on her good leg for a pat and licked her hand.

That night, half asleep in the barn, Liv heard Diego snort and whinny in the corral. Sleepily, she got to her feet and turned on the light. Cactus Jack's ears were pricked forward, and he stamped uneasily in the stall.

"What is it, Jack? What's wrong?" Liv peered through the dusty window. There was somebody out there! She could see movement among the milling horses.

Liv slid the window open. "Hey!" she shouted into the night air. "Who's there?"

Thudding footsteps and then the sound of a low, throttled motor told her she had frightened off whoever had upset the horses. Liv shoved her arms into her jacket sleeves and slipped out of the barn. A quick check told her Diego and the rest of the herd were okay. Diego snuffled and nudged her shoulder with his long nose. "Good boy!" she told the big stallion. "We scared them off, didn't we?"

What were they after, she wondered as she retraced her steps to her bed of straw and saddle blankets outside Cactus Jack's stall. Could they be trying to steal Diego or some of the other horses? If only Shane had stayed, he might have caught those men and asked them some questions. Suddenly the Lucky Star Ranch felt isolated and lonely in the dark desert night. Once more she tossed and turned restlessly, waiting for morning.

14
SHANE'S DREAM

Liv woke achingly stiff from her night in the barn. She needed to check for signs of invaders in the corral first thing. "Jack," she called, "how're you doin'?"

Cactus Jack stuck his nose over the stall door and blew softly to let her know he was hungry. "All right," Liv said, struggling to her feet. "I'll get you some hay and water while I'm looking for tracks."

But Liv could find no traces of boot treads in the corral, and if there were ATV tracks, she couldn't tell them apart from the truck's. If the coyotes had paid a visit, the horses had trampled the evidence into dust. Sighing, Liv broke off a flake of hay for Cactus Jack and filled his water pail. She'd search again once he was fed and watered.

As she limped back to the barn, Liv saw Sophie framed in the open doorway. Her halo of fine hair stood out around her face, lit by the morning sun. Liv felt a pang of regret for all that had happened between them in the past weeks.

"You look awful," Sophie said. "How's Jack?"

"Okay," Liv grunted. "I'm just going to feed him." She felt her sore knee buckle.

"Let me." Sophie ran to take the hay and water bucket. "Go get some breakfast—it's late—almost time for the bus."

"Oh!" Liv slumped against the barn door. "The bus? School? I can't!"

"I know it's hard with all the kids talking about you, and Shane," Sophie sympathized. "If you only wouldn't let your feelings show so much."

"That's not all," Liv groaned. "Shane's not coming until tonight, and I need to walk Cactus Jack today."

"Come on, then." Sophie reached out her hand to Liv. "Let's go try to convince Mom to let you stay home again. But it's going to be a hard sell."

Liv stood for a second, holding Sophie's hand. "I've made a mess of things, haven't I?" she said wearily. "And it's too late to fix them." She glanced at her grandfather's horse feed calendar on the wall. "Look! Gran and Granddad will be home a week from tomorrow. We'll be leaving . . ." Her slim shoulders sagged.

"You're hungry and tired." Sophie gently pulled her forward. "Things will look better after some bacon and eggs."

Liv's stomach suddenly churned. "No, they won't." She looked back at Cactus Jack. "I'll be leaving him, too."

Jess reluctantly agreed to let Liv stay home. She looked pityingly at her stubborn daughter. "But this is the *last* time," she insisted. "Don't think for one minute it's going to be this easy to skip school once we're back in Vancouver."

As they watched Sophie run for the bus twenty minutes later, Jess put her arm around Liv's shoulders and gave her a squeeze. "You've had a tough time with Cactus Jack getting hurt," she said.

"But please! Don't overdo it with that horse. I don't want you getting sick with a big trip ahead of us."

Liv could only nod miserably. In her mother's mind, they had already packed and left.

"And who will care if I do leave?" she asked Cactus Jack as she led him out to join the other horses in the big corral.

Cactus Jack whickered in sympathy.

"Shane's going to be glad to get rid of me, that's for sure," Liv went on. "Cheyenne will be thrilled. And the rest of the kids at school won't even notice I'm gone." For some reason she thought of Brady's cheerful, goofy face. "Well, there's *one* guy who might miss me."

Cactus Jack bobbed his head. "You haven't even met Brady!" laughed Liv. "Don't pretend you know him." But she loved the way Jack seemed to understand what she was thinking.

The Lucky Star horses were gathered under the oak trees on the shady side of the corral. Diego came out to meet Cactus Jack, to stretch his neck over Jack's and welcome him back officially to the herd. Cisco came to welcome him, too, with a swish of his tail and a low whinny. Cactus Jack bobbed his head as if to say he was glad to be part of the group again.

"Come on—we have work to do." Liv firmly tugged him away. "Walking until you're not so sore. Shane will be riding you again in a few days."

At the thought of Shane, Liv remembered that she should be looking for signs the coyotes had been there. She scanned the ground carefully as she walked Jack around the corral but saw nothing. "I'll tell Shane about the noises and the movements I saw anyway," she promised herself. "Even if he doesn't want to talk to me, he'll want to hear about that."

Shane waved off Liv's fears about the coyotes with a swish of his hat. "If those dudes come back, I'll hear them. Don't worry." He examined Cactus Jack's wound and took his temperature. "Normal. The antibiotic has definitely kicked in."

"I hope so," Liv said. "Well—good night. Thanks for coming."

"You don't have to thank me." Shane looked away. "It's my fault Cactus Jack is in this fix. I should never have rode him in the rodeo. I'll take good care of him—after you're gone."

Liv didn't know what to say. She kissed Cactus Jack's nose and walked away, trying not to limp.

Her mother and sister were sitting in the kitchen when she came in.

"Want some hot chocolate?" Jess smiled at her.

"No, thanks," Liv said, leaning on the door frame. "I'm going to bed." She was suddenly so tired her head was swimming. "I think I'll sleep in Gran's room so I don't have to climb the stairs."

Her grandmother's bed was warm and soft. "It's all right," Liv told herself as she settled in. "Shane will look after the horses." She was asleep before she could count to ten.

Shane, sleeping in the barn, dreamed he was on a cattle roundup in Wild Horse Creek Canyon. The red rock walls towered above him. A bright campfire burned at his feet. The dream was so real he could smell the wood smoke. Tux ran in circles, barking at the cows. Shane tried to yank on his cowboy boots so he could go quiet the dog, but they were too small . . . He gave up and fell back into a deep sleep.

When he woke at dawn, Tux was staring at him with his head on his paws. "All right," Shane groaned, "I'm getting up." A quick check on Cactus Jack told him all was well. It was time to feed and water the horses in the corral. As Shane struggled into his boots, his dream returned in a rush. Why had he been trying to get those boots on?

Outside, spreading hay for the horses, he spotted a scorched patch on the ground. Tux whined and dug at the sandy soil as if he was digging for a bone.

"What you got there?" Shane sat on his heels to look.

Tux held a short length of iron bar in his jaws.

"Shane?"

He looked up to see Liv standing behind him.

"Looks like we had visitors again last night," he muttered. "Give me that, Tux. Good dog." He turned the iron bar over in his hands. "This here's a branding iron. Somebody set up a portable forge so they could get it red hot. I smelled smoke but I thought I was dreaming."

"What were they going to do with it?" Liv bent closer to look.

"Sometimes horse thieves try to change a brand." He ran his fingers over the wide end of the iron bar. "See here? It's shaped like the letter *B*. If you put this over the Lucky Star brand, the *L* turns into *B*." He traced the letters in the sand so Liv could see.

"They were trying to steal our horses?" Liv gasped.

Shane squinted up at her. "Most likely Diego. The coyotes prefer stallions. Tux must have scared them off, barking. I heard that in my dream, too." Shane stroked the dog's head thoughtfully. "I think I'll do some lookin' around. See if I can follow their tracks. I'll leave Tux here . . . just in case."

Liv knew Shane was an expert tracker. He could find marks in the desert sand no one else would notice. "You won't do anything dangerous?" she asked, then realized from the look on Shane's face that she was showing her feelings again. "I mean, okay, I'll keep Tux in the barn for you."

"I'll be goin' then." Shane strode toward Navajo, his saddle in his arms. "I haven't given Cactus Jack his shot yet," he called over his shoulder.

"I can do it!" Liv shouted after him. As Shane rode away minutes later, Tux struggled against Liv's hold on his collar. He whined deep in his throat. "I know, fella," Liv gulped. "We're both scared for him. Where is he going that he wouldn't take you? If he meets up with those coyotes . . ."

She shut Tux in a stall while she prepared the injection for Cactus Jack the way the vet had shown them. She thumped the skin on his hindquarters with the heel of her hand and then slipped in the needle. Cactus Jack didn't seem to feel it. He stood still while she slowly depressed the plunger until the syringe was empty.

"Good boy, good Jack," she breathed, smoothing the skin over the site. "You get a treat for that." She was holding out a carrot for him to chomp when she heard fast footsteps coming down the plank floor.

"Liv!" It was Sophie, her face red and her hair standing out around it. "You have to come quick."

"Don't worry." Liv looked at her watch. "We have half an hour before the bus gets here."

"Not the bus . . . ," Sophie gasped. "Mom got a call . . . from the hospital."

Liv gripped the carrot in her hand. "Gran."

"No." Sophie brushed tears from her cheeks. "Not Gran. It's Granddad. He had a heart attack."

15
TAKING CHANCES

Both girls headed for the house, Sophie running and Liv limping as fast as she could.

Their mother's face was pale. "We have to get to Tucson—right now!" She looked around wildly. "Where's Shane?"

"He already left," Liv said, wishing with all her heart that he hadn't.

"Then we'll have to call him from the hospital and tell him to come back after school to look after the horses. Hurry, girls!"

"Is Granddad—?" Liv gulped.

"No, he . . . survived, but the emergency department advised me to come as soon as possible." Jess reached for her handbag and pulled out sunglasses and keys.

"Mom!" Liv seized her mother's arm. "I can't leave Cactus Jack. I—I have to give him his injections and keep an eye on him and I don't know when Shane will get here." She knew she sounded selfish and horse-crazy, but she couldn't tell Mom how worried she was about Shane, too. There was no time to go into all that!

Jess stood very still. "I don't know what to do. I have to go." Her eyes searched their faces. "Can I trust you to stay by yourselves? To go to school today and come straight back to the ranch? Cactus Jack will be all right on his own for a few hours, and you can call the vet for help if Shane doesn't show up. I'll be back as fast as I can. Most likely tonight."

Liv nodded. "I'll be fine." She gulped. "Tell Granddad I love him."

"I don't have to stay, too, do I?" Sophie pleaded.

Jess nodded. "I'd feel better knowing you were together—two heads are better than one."

Sophie threw her arms around her mother. "Poor Granddad," she murmured. "All this time we've been worried about Gran when he was the one . . ."

"Yes," Jess said. "That's how it happens sometimes." She paused, then shook her head. "Come on. I'll drop you at school on my way through town."

"What's wrong?" Brady's worried face peered down into Liv's an hour later. He was handing out test papers and had paused beside her desk. As he bent lower, the stack slid out of his grasp and cascaded to the floor at her feet.

Laughter erupted around the classroom. "Sorry," Brady apologized. "But you look so worried! Can I help . . . with anything?"

Liv ignored the laughter. She bent to help him scoop up the papers. "My grandfather . . . ," she started and then bit her lip. Mom's last instruction had been not to tell anyone they were alone at the ranch in case she didn't make it back that night. It made sense, the way news spread in Rattlesnake Bend. To Brady she whispered, "I'll talk to you at lunch."

Maybe Brady would have an idea where Shane had gone.

"There've been some guys snooping around our ranch lately," she explained to him when they were alone on the bench outside the school. The noon sun blazed down beyond the sharp line of shade provided by the school building. Brady sat beside her, the crumbs from his muffin falling in her lap. For once she didn't notice his clumsiness. His face was close to hers.

"They might be horse thieves," she said. "Shane went looking for them and left his dog at our ranch. I think that means he was going someplace really dangerous."

Brady shrugged his broad shoulders. "Any idea where he was headed?"

Liv thought for a moment. "Yes! The first time I saw those men, they were camped out in the Heartbreak Hills to the west of our place. Shane saw their campfire, too."

"Oh!" Brady's blue eyes widened. "They could be holed up in that ghost town. What do you want to do? Tell the border police?"

"I already called them on my cell this morning and left a message," Liv told him. "But what if nobody takes it seriously? I'm scared Shane won't be back when I get home after school . . . Would you ride out there with me and look for him?"

"But you can't ride," Brady said. "Your knee."

Liv undid her brace and flexed her leg cautiously. "The doc said I could ride by next week," she told him. "It feels okay now."

Brady stared for a minute. "And you'd like me—*me*—to ride up to Heartbreak with you?"

"Would you?" Liv glanced at him.

"Sure!" Brady's face lit up. "My horse, Ginger, is a great trail horse." He thought a moment. "Instead of ridin' all the way out to your ranch, I could meet you where the Cow Creek Road joins the track up to Heartbreak. I'll wait for you there at four-thirty. Can you make it by then?"

"I'll be there," Liv agreed. "Thanks, Brady."

"Where are you going?" Sophie demanded as she watched Liv heave a saddle on a small bay mare called Trixie. "You can't ride." It was stiflingly hot in the afternoon sun.

"I'm going to meet Brady Bolt," Liv told her. It wasn't a lie. And she had to hurry if she was going to reach their meeting place by four-thirty.

"Brady!" Sophie's eyes widened. "What for?"

"Doesn't matter." Liv limped back to the corral rail for Trixie's bridle. "I gave Cactus Jack his antibiotic. I'll be back before dark—if Mom gets home, tell her not to worry."

"I'm not letting you go riding alone. I'm coming with you," Sophie insisted.

"Don't." Liv didn't meet her stare. "Stay here and wait for Mom. She'll freak if no one's here. And keep an eye on Jack for me. Make sure he drinks."

Sophie brushed back her fine hair and settled her hat firmly on her head. "Something's up," she said. "It's no use telling me there isn't. Anyway, Mom wouldn't want me to let you go by yourself."

"I'm not going to be by myself. I'm meeting Brady." Liv led Trixie to the fence, climbed a rail, stuck her left foot in the stirrup and swung her leg over the saddle. Her knee protested, but it wasn't a sharp pain. "Stay here," she repeated, looking at Sophie for the first time.

"It's something about Shane!" Sophie gasped. "I can see it in your face as if it was written in great big neon lights. That's it. I'm coming, too."

Liv groaned. This was the worst thing about being twins—Sophie could always read her face. She wheeled Trixie away from the fence and jogged off to the west. "Don't forget to bring a canteen of water!" she shouted back over her shoulder.

RIDING AT LAST!

Liv felt a surge of happiness as Trixie stretched into an easy jog toward the Heartbreak Hills. Despite everything—her worry about Granddad and Shane, the nagging pain in her knee—she was riding again at last. Riding over the open desert, moving to the rhythm of a horse's body. Horses didn't reject you because you were too young. Horses didn't hate you because you liked somebody they thought belonged to them!

You couldn't fool a horse, Liv thought, or put on an act to impress them. They just accepted you the way you were. Maybe she sometimes acted without thinking—maybe she was even reckless at times. And maybe her emotions *did* show on her face. That didn't bother Trixie. The little mare picked up speed, loving to run on a long, loose rein.

Sophie caught up as Liv was approaching the junction where Brady was waiting.

"Liv, stop! Wait!" She sounded desperate.

Liv slowed Trixie to a walk. "You didn't have to come. You could have stayed and waited for Mom and looked after Cactus Jack."

"Never mind that. Listen, I've been trying to catch you to tell you . . ." Sophie gasped for breath. "I had to go to the far end of the corral to get Cisco . . . Diego was gone!"

Liv slumped forward in the saddle. She clutched Trixie's black mane. "Granddad's horse—his heart will break if anything happens to him. We've got to get him back!"

"But you're not surprised he's gone." Sophie wheeled Cisco around so she could stare into Liv's face. "What's going on?"

"I'll explain as we ride." As they rode side by side to meet Brady, Liv told Sophie how she stumbled across the coyotes in the desert the day of her accident, about the noises in the night, Shane finding the branding iron and riding off without Tux.

Brady was waiting in the shade of an oak tree on Ginger, a tall chestnut mare with a white snip on her nose. Liv quickly told him about Diego being stolen. "If the coyotes have Diego, I know Shane will try to rescue him," Liv said. She turned to Sophie. "He might track the smugglers to Heartbreak. He and Brady both said the ghost town could be their hideout."

Sophie shivered. "Shane's in danger. All this has been going on for days—people hanging around the ranch—and you never told me?"

Liv just looked at her. It was useless to say they hadn't exactly been communicating lately. "Do you know how long it will take us to get there?" she asked Brady.

"Won't take much more than an hour." He glanced doubtfully at Liv's knee. "Are you sure you can ride that far?"

"I'm sure," Liv said. "Let's go."

Brady looked different on a horse, she thought. He sat tall in the saddle, his hands the practiced hands of someone used to riding—

one holding the reins, the other resting on the saddle horn. He didn't seem young or clumsy as he led them up the trail.

"Shouldn't we tell someone where we're going?" Sophie called from behind.

"My folks know," Brady called back. "I didn't tell them all the details, but if we're not back by sundown, they'll know where to look."

"What did you tell them?" Liv was curious.

"Oh, just that I was goin' riding with a girl from school." Brady turned with his mischievous grin. "A girl who finally decided I wasn't *so* bad."

"You're not bad at all." Liv couldn't help smiling back. "I'm really glad you're here." She was surprised at how totally she meant her words.

The afternoon heat waves shimmered up from the trail ahead, but as they climbed into the hills, the air was fresher. It was a steep climb, up a series of switchbacks. Liv knew Sophie would be nervous of the heights, and it didn't help when Brady called a halt on a jutting ledge overlooking a steep drop.

"This used to be the road to Heartbreak Mine and the town," he told them. "If you look down there, you can see wrecks of cars and trucks. A long time ago, before cars had air conditioning, everybody drove these desert roads at night to escape the heat. Some didn't make this curve—spun off the road and rolled."

They could just make out the rusted hulks of metal far below on the barren slope. "Heartbreak was a pretty big town," Brady went on. "Movie stars from Hollywood used to come up here to get married in the hotel."

"What happened to it?" Sophie asked.

"Silver played out, I guess." Brady shrugged. "Everybody left— just shut her down and walked away. There used to be excursions up here to visit the ghost town, but then the road got too bad."

"And too risky." Sophie pointed to a sign:

TRAVEL CAUTION

SMUGGLING AND ILLEGAL

IMMIGRATION MAY BE

ENCOUNTERED IN THIS AREA

"Not all illegal immigrants are bad people," Liv said, swinging Cactus Jack's head back to the trail. "Some of them are refugees." She was thinking about Temo's cousin.

Brady agreed. "I know that, but the border country is still a pretty rough place."

"There's a sign we're getting close to Heartbreak." Brady pointed to white-and-brown patches moving through the dry hillside brush. "Wild *burros*."

Sophie and Liv watched as a long-eared mare and her tiny snow-white foal stepped out of the bushes.

"They're adorable!" Sophie cried, leaning down for a better look.

Brady said, "They're hungry. If we got off our horses, they'd come right up to us, beggin' for food."

"Who looks after them?" Sophie asked.

"They look after themselves, pretty well," Brady told her. "The miners used them to haul silver, and when they closed the mine, they let them run wild."

"You mean they abandoned them!" Sophie was outraged.

"The *burros* manage to survive somehow," said Brady with a shrug. "And they're protected up here on government land."

"We have to get going." Liv glanced at her watch. "It's already after five."

As they rode on, Sophie looked back over her shoulder at the *burros*. The place was so lonely and wild—how could they survive?

There were soon more signs of human activity from long ago. Slashes in the hillside, abandoned shacks with gaping windows, crumpled heaps of metal.

And then, around a corner, the main street of Heartbreak appeared in a narrow canyon, gashed like a wound in the hills. Old buildings clung to the steep hillsides, one almost on top of the other. Twisted wooden stairways connected them to the street below.

"There's the hotel." Brady pointed. At the end of the gulch, the end of the short main street, stood the ramshackle remains of the Heartbreak Hotel. It was three stories high, with two wooden balconies running across the front. Now the roof and parts of the balconies sagged at weird angles. The once-bright paint had worn to desert gray.

As they rode closer, their horses' feet echoed from the rock walls on either side. Sophie could see why it was a perfect hideout. Nobody could reach the back of the hotel, which was built into the rock. And no one could approach the front without being heard.

Maybe the smugglers were in there right now, watching through broken windows, waiting for them. Sophie wanted to turn Cisco and run. But Diego might be somewhere close, and maybe Shane. She glanced at Liv, riding beside her. Liv leaned forward eagerly, her face flushed with excitement. If only she could be as fearless, Sophie wished, just this once.

17
HEARTBREAK HOTEL

The crumbling steps creaked as they climbed to the hotel's entrance. Huge, round pillars framed the large front door. Inside, more pillars supported a high-domed ceiling.

Liv and Sophie stared around in amazement. Golden angels and flying birds floated above them. Carved plaster scrolls decorated each pillar. Along one whole side of the room stretched an enormous gilded bar, with ceiling-high mirrors behind it.

"I told you it was fancy," Brady said into the hushed silence. "This was the Heartbreak Saloon." The gold was chipping off the ceiling and the pillars holding up the second floor, but it was clear, even in the dim light, that this had been a magnificent room.

"What a spooky old place," Liv whispered. "You can almost hear the ghosts of the miners and movie stars moaning."

"That groan was no ghost!" Brady cried. "Somebody's here."

He dived behind the end of the bar. "Come quick!" he shouted. "It's Shane!"

Shane lay crumpled behind the bar.

"Don't move him," Liv urged. "Not till we know where he's hurt."

"Can't see in this light." Brady bent closer.

Just then, Shane groaned again and tried to sit up. He raised his hand to his forehead. "Un-uh! Feels . . . someone dropped a cement block on me. Gotta move . . . 'fore they come back . . ."

"How long have you been lying here?" asked Liv.

"Don't know. I—I've been driftin' in and out."

"Come on," Liv said, "we're going to help you out from behind the bar."

Once Shane was in the light, they could see that his face was pasty gray. A lump the size of a tennis ball was turning purple on his forehead.

"Who did this?" Sophie cried. "Who hit you?"

Shane looked puzzled, as though he was playing a movie in his head that didn't make sense. "The coyotes," he gasped. "Got to stop them, they've got Diego, tell the girls . . ."

"We're right here!" Sophie seized his hand.

"Sophie! You're all right." A silly grin spread across Shane's swollen face as he collapsed back to the floor. "I'm sure glad to see *you*."

At that second, Liv knew he cared more about Sophie than he ever let on. But strangely, it didn't hurt as much as she'd expected. Maybe Sophie had been right and it was mostly hero worship she'd been feeling. She had no time to think about it now. The important thing was to get Shane out of here—fast. "Where are the coyotes now?" she begged him to concentrate. "Think. Are they here in the hotel?"

Shane propped himself up on one elbow, trying to focus his scattered thoughts. "No. Before they knocked me out . . . border control came through . . . lookin' for them. They must've taken off, but they'll be back . . . Got Diego in a trailer on the other side of the hill. Got another stallion upstairs." He pointed vaguely to the ceiling. "He's a wild one. I can hear him stamping and crashing around—enough to bring the roof down."

They all looked up. There was no sound. "He must be delirious," Liv whispered to Brady. "There can't be a horse up there."

"Maybe there can," Brady said quickly. "In the silver rush days, guys used to ride their horses right into this saloon, load them in a freight elevator back there . . ." He pointed to the rear of the cavernous room. "Upstairs they had a livery stable with stalls and hay and a blacksmith's shop built right into the rock."

Brady didn't get any further. A loud stamping brought part of the golden ceiling smashing to the floor.

"Told you," Shane moaned. "He's up there, like Brady says."

"What do they want stallions for?" Sophie asked, grabbing Shane's hand again.

"Stallion fights." Brady gave a disgusted snort. "People pay a lot of money to see horses fight to the death in some places. Bet money on it."

"That's sickening!" Liv gasped. "Those men are capturing stallions like Diego for fighting?"

"They're bad men." Shane struggled to stand up. "There're three of them—on an ATV. Got to get you girls out. Where're your horses?"

"Tied them to a rail back down the street." Sophie took his weight on her shoulder. "Come on, we'll help you walk."

"Wait!" Liv grabbed her arm. "We can't go and leave Diego and that other stallion upstairs."

"That stallion's wild, and crazy," Shane said. "Might not be easy . . ."

"Anyway"—Sophie faced Liv with a flaming face—"the important thing is Shane. We'll have to worry about the horses later!"

Another fit of pounding shook the building. Liv glanced up. "We might not have time. Sophie, you and Brady get Shane out of here and on his horse. I'm going to try to free both stallions. Don't wait for me."

"I'll come with you." Brady took Liv's hand. "I think there's a back way through the second floor to where they've stashed Diego. We can get both horses out that way."

"Please don't go and leave us here," begged Sophie.

"If they can save Diego!" Shane's voice was hoarse. "Sophie, he's your granddad's favorite—his partner. Let them try."

Sophie and Liv exchanged anguished glances. Shane didn't know how important it was—they hadn't told him about Granddad's heart attack. "All right." Sophie gave in. "But hurry!"

Liv and Brady struggled up the sagging stairs to the second floor. "The back of the hotel butts up against the hill," puffed Brady. "Supposed to be a tunnel through to the other side. I'll bet that's where they have a truck and trailer with Diego. There's a track from there leads into Mexico."

They sped down the wide hall. The shattering noise of the stallion's frantic kicking surrounded them. Liv could feel the whole building shake as she reached for the stable door at the hall's end.

"Wait!" Brady held Liv back. "First, we should find the tunnel entrance."

"You're not scared of the stallion, are you?" Liv stared at him.

"No, but if we're gonna get him out that way, we'd better know where it is." Brady's face was pale. "Like Shane says, I don't think it'll be easy to control him."

"Right." Liv sucked in a deep breath. "So let's find the tunnel. Any ideas?"

"All I know is it was a secret exit for rustlers and thieves, or somebody who'd lost too much playin' poker downstairs. My dad told me all about this place."

Liv scanned the doorways along the corridor. Besides the stable door there was one marked "Office." She turned the wobbly handle. The room was empty, with scattered papers, yellow with age, on shelves, desks and the floor.

"What a mess!" Brady breathed.

"Yeah, but look!" Liv pointed to smudges on the strewn papers leading to a closet door. "Footprints—coming from there!"

Brady ran to the door and pulled on the handle. It gave way so suddenly he fell backward, flattening Liv. "Sorry, sorry!" he apologized in an agonized voice. "Did I hurt your knee?"

"It's okay." Liv squirmed out from under him. "Look! You've found it." A blast of cool, damp air came from the doorway. A tunnel stretched away into the rock.

They glanced at each other across the dusty floor. Brady reached out to wipe a smudge of dirt off Liv's cheek. He gazed into her eyes, his forehead crinkled with concern. "You sure you . . . want to go in there?" he faltered. "It looks so . . . dark."

"I'm okay." Liv scrambled to her feet. "I'll go search for the smugglers' truck and Diego. You've got the hard part—the other stallion. Try to calm him, keep him from bringing down the roof and killing us all."

18

STALLION'S REVENGE

As she limped down the tunnel's dark length, feeling for the sides, Liv's mind flashed back to Shane's story about the girl who'd died in the mine shaft at Heartbreak. What if this tunnel caved in on her? It was very old . . .

She moved toward a sliver of light. At the end of the passage, an old-fashioned two-horse trailer blocked the exit. The coyotes must have parked it there so they could load the other stallion without risking his getting loose.

"Diego!" Liv shouted, seeing a black tail and blue roan rear end filling one side. "Oh, you poor horse!"

Diego kicked and stormed his loud dislike at being shut in a trailer in the hot sun. "How am I going to do this?" Liv shoved helplessly at the wedged trailer. "I want you free to run back to the ranch, not shut in this tunnel with me."

She hopped into the empty side of the trailer and out its small front opening to the narrow desert track. The sun and open air were a shock after the dark. The horse trailer was attached to a pickup truck perched on the side of a high, steep hill. The track led down the hill and away across the desert to the Sierra Madre mountains in the south.

"Please let the truck be unlocked," Liv begged. It was, but the keys weren't in it. How could she move it? Suddenly she remembered that Granddad had warned them never to fool around with the gears in his truck. It could start to roll if it was in neutral.

As she moved the gear lever, the truck made a small crunching movement on the gravel. It might work! Liv hauled herself out of the cab, back through the trailer. She unloaded Diego into the tunnel, where he snorted and fussed at finding himself still shut in.

"Just for a second, boy," she told him. "I have to get the truck out of your way."

Back in the pickup, Liv eased off the emergency brake. Immediately, the truck started to roll. She yanked on the brake, but the heavy vehicle was gathering speed. There was no choice. Liv opened the door and half fell, half jumped out.

Just in time! She threw herself back as the truck and trailer sped down the steep incline. Liv watched them go, the trailer swinging on its hitch, bouncing over rocks. Finally they left the track and hurtled down the hillside out of sight. Liv heard a terrible crash somewhere far below. She stood with her hand over her mouth and then felt a nudge on her shoulder. It was Diego, standing behind her, looking down at the spot where the truck and trailer had disappeared.

Liv turned to stroke Diego's long, intelligent face. "Run like the wind," she told him. "Back to the Lucky Star. Go! Now!"

Diego gave a long, loud neigh and started down the steep hill at top speed.

"Now for the other stallion." Liv took her last breath of clear desert air and headed back through the tunnel to the Heartbreak Hotel. As she approached, the thunder of the stallion's kicking echoed through the rocks. Brady was in the stable!

At the same moment, Liv heard the roar of a large ATV echoing off the canyon walls of Heartbreak's main street. The coyotes were back! They would burst into the hotel at any minute.

Liv limped to the stable door and yanked it open. "Quick!" she roared at Brady. "Let him out of the stall!"

Brady's face was white. He wrenched back the bolt on the stall door and jumped out of the way as the stallion, his pent-up fury finally released, stormed out.

"It's him!" Liv shouted, stunned. "The black stallion that attacked Diego!" There was no mistaking the white blaze down his nose or his four white socks, his proud, high-arching neck, battle scarred. Liv remembered the wild horse streaking across the desert floor, his plumed tail flying high, running for his life. Now she was close enough to see the whites of his eyes, the flicking of his ears, hear his loud snorting breath as he fought for escape.

"Watch out!" Liv yelled. Brady leaped back just as the stallion kicked high and thundered out of the stable. They tore after him— heard him pounding down the wide staircase, heard the cracking and splintering of the old stairs under his hooves.

As he galloped across the saloon, the hotel door opened and the three coyotes stood gaping at the onrushing horse. The stallion's ears flattened to his skull. He recognized his enemies.

He charged. One of the men turned and fled out the door. The other two dived behind the bar. The black stallion reared and struck at the polished surface, smashing it to pieces. The smugglers crawled deeper under the solid wood for refuge.

"That *diablo*!" one of them shouted. "A fighter to the end. He'd be worth thousands!"

A huge chunk of a pillar crashed to the floor.

"Never mind him, you fool!" the other man howled. "We've still got the blue roan from the ranch. Let's get out of here while we can." The two men raced for the open door and took a flying jump from the veranda.

Liv half threw herself down the shattered stairs. Sophie and Shane were there somewhere, helpless in the stallion's path.

"He's going to bring the place down!" Brady shouted. "Let's get out of here!"

"I can't!" Liv howled. "I have to find Sophie and Shane!" In the dust and confusion below, they had vanished. This was too much like Shane's story of the cave-in. Like a nightmare happening before her eyes.

Brady half lifted, half dragged Liv across the lobby toward the door. She struggled against him. "SOPHIE!" she screamed.

They made it down the steps and into the street just as the top floors of the Heartbreak Hotel collapsed. The black stallion blasted past them, crushing the stairs behind him.

"SOPHIE!" Liv shouted in anguish.

She stared at the hotel's ruined remains. Dust rose from the pile of broken beams and shattered windows. Somewhere, under there . . .

"This is all my fault," she sobbed into Brady's chest. "My sister! And Shane! I should be in there, too. Why didn't you let me stay?"

Brady awkwardly wrapped Liv in his arms and held her tight. "Couldn't," he mumbled. "Had to get you out. Sorry." Then he gave her a sudden hard hug. "And good thing I did, because, look!" He gently turned her around.

Coming from the end of the collapsed veranda was a dust-covered Sophie, holding up a limping Shane. Brady rushed forward to support him while Sophie and Liv ran to each other and locked in a tight embrace. "You're all right!" they cried together.

"I was so scared." Liv stared into her twin's face as if she could never get enough of looking at her. "I thought, I thought . . ."

"I got Shane out as the smugglers were coming up the street," Sophie explained, her eyes bright. She looked in awe at the hotel. "What happened?"

"The wild stallion," Liv said slowly. "He had a score to settle. He was our black stallion—the one who fought Diego. Only in Wild Horse Creek Canyon it wasn't a fight to the death."

"Where did he go?" Shane asked. "I'd give a lot to see that horse again!"

"He disappeared down the road after the coyotes." Brady pointed. "He's probably still chasing those guys on their ATV."

"We never even really saw their faces!" Liv exclaimed.

"Just like real coyotes," Brady said. "They come and go like shadows."

Sophie took Shane's hand. "What did they hit you with?" she asked. "It made an awful dent." The bump on his head had spread to one eye, giving him a lopsided look.

"That darned branding iron Tux found in the corral." Shane tried to grin at Sophie. "Guess it could have been worse. They could have got it red hot first." He swallowed hard. "It was stupid to bring it with me. As soon as they saw it, they knew I was from the Lucky Star Ranch. They couldn't afford to let me go." He paused. The pain in his eyes was not from his head wound. "But they've got Diego."

"No, they don't. He's free." Liv brushed back the hair from her eyes. "But I'm afraid the coyotes' truck went for a ride down the hill with nobody in it. Right now I'll bet it looks like those wrecks we saw on the way up to Heartbreak."

"Then we shouldn't stand around talkin'," Shane warned. "When those guys find out they've lost Diego and their transport, they're going to be back for us."

"Our horses are tied down the street." Liv shuddered at the thought of the men returning. "Where's Navajo?"

"I stashed him somewhere safe," Shane told them. "In the old privies at the end of town."

"He's in an outhouse? A washroom?" Sophie stared.

"Navajo won't mind." Shane tried to grin again. "Nobody's used them for years."

19
AFTERSHOCKS

"Are you sure you can ride?" Sophie asked Shane when they had rescued Navajo from the old wooden building. The buckskin paint stood patiently, waiting for Shane to mount.

"Don't worry, Navajo will take care of me," Shane promised, but Sophie could see he was weak as he struggled into the saddle. Usually, watching Shane getting on a horse was like watching one perfect fluid motion that required no effort at all.

"I'll be all right once I get back to my trailer," he muttered. "It's Friday . . . no school tomorrow."

"We're not letting you stay at that lonesome place by yourself," Liv protested.

"You're coming to the ranch with us," Sophie added. "I'm going to look after you."

"Come on, girls," Shane groaned. "Don't start . . ."

"It's all right." Liv tossed her head. "Sophie and I won't be fighting over you anymore. Brady and I are together now." She gave him a quick glance. "If that's okay with you, Brady?"

"You mean it?" Brady looked astonished, then a grin spread from ear to ear. "Hey, yeah! It's okay with me."

"Good. Then help me up on Trixie and let's go." Liv mounted the mare with a boost from Brady. "Back to the Lucky Star."

Sophie stared in astonishment at her sister. Whether Liv meant it or not, she was very convincing.

"All right . . . I guess." Shane still sounded woozy. "I'd like to come to the ranch . . . get Tux and make sure Diego made it back. Your granddad would be awful upset if anything happened to his horse."

Sophie froze with her foot in Cisco's stirrup. Granddad! They'd have to tell Shane the bad news—once he was safe at the ranch.

The sun was setting over the Heartbreak Hills as they rode down the trail. Ahead, they could just spot the taillights of the smugglers' ATV. At the junction, where the trail met the road, other lights appeared, one flashing red.

"Hey! That's the border patrol!" Brady cheered. "Those coyotes didn't get far."

The lights were on at the Lucky Star Ranch when the four rode into the yard. A quick check of the corral showed them Diego was quietly munching hay—he must have jumped the fence to join his herd. As they got off their horses, he lifted his head and snorted as if to say, "It's about time you got here!"

They could hear Tux barking in the barn. Sophie ran to let him out. The border collie dashed in and out of Navajo's legs, yapping madly until Shane gathered him up in his arms.

"Mom's back, too." Sophie sucked in her breath at the sight of Jess's silver van parked outside the house.

They left their horses in the yard and headed for the house. Jess came to the door as they crossed the veranda. They all saw the shock on her face as she took in their appearance—Shane with his bruised face, Brady suddenly part of the group, all of them dusty and weary.

"What happened? Wh-where have you been?" she stammered.

"How's Granddad?" Liv burst out.

"He's still in the hospital, in Tucson. The doctors say he's out of danger but he'll need bypass surgery."

Beside her, Sophie felt Shane's knees buckle. "Your granddad . . . Ted . . . is sick?" he mumbled the fearful question.

"Granddad had a heart attack today," Sophie whispered. "We were going to tell you."

Their mother passed an exhausted hand over her forehead. "I trusted you girls to look after things while I was gone, but you weren't here when I got back, and you all seem to have gone on some kind of wild ride."

"We can explain, Mom," Liv said. "We *were* looking after things, I promise."

"Later"—Jess held up her hand—"I brought your grandmother home. Clean up a bit before you see her. She doesn't need any more worry tonight."

"I'll take Shane to the kitchen," Sophie said quickly.

"Brady and I will get the horses settled." Liv nodded. "Meet you back here." She and Brady set off across the yard.

"I'm real sorry about your grandfather," Brady said. "Everybody around here thinks Ted Starr and your grandmother are great. They're like . . . legends."

"He's *got* to get better," Liv stormed. "All this time we were worried about Gran and nobody realized Granddad was"—her voice stuck in her throat—"so sick himself."

They unsaddled Trixie, Navajo and Cisco, brushed them down and spread hay for them in the corral. Liv took Cactus Jack's temperature, felt his legs and back and gave him his final antibiotic injection. "You seem fine," she sighed, hugging him. "You're my brave, tough, wonderful Cactus Jack."

"I should be goin' before it gets too much darker—my folks will be worried." Brady held out his hand. "But I'll see you at school on Monday, or maybe sooner."

He hadn't said anything about her outburst back at Heartbreak, Liv thought, as they shut Cactus Jack's stall and walked back to the yard, where he'd tied Ginger. Maybe she'd just embarrassed him by suggesting they were a couple.

"Thanks for getting me out of the hotel up there," she said, shuddering at the memory of the ruined building. "You were great."

Brady swung up into Ginger's saddle and looked down at her with a worried expression. "I hope I didn't hurt you haulin' on you like that," he said. "It's the first time I ever tried to pick up a girl—you're heavier than you look!"

"Thanks a lot!" Liv laughed.

"Oh! Sorry, I didn't mean . . . !" Brady's face grew red.

"It's okay. I know what you mean. See you later." That's the old Brady, Liv thought, awkward even with his words. Watching him ride out of the yard, she felt a strange sensation steal over her. Not the feeling she'd had about Temo, or even Shane. This was different—not so exciting or dizzying, but better, more real.

She waited till he turned and waved, knowing he would, and then walked slowly toward the house, her mind already working on a new plan to stay at the Lucky Star Ranch. They couldn't leave now.

Cleaned up, changed and with a plate of snacks on the table and cold drinks in their hands, Liv, Sophie and Shane listened to Gran tell them about Ted Starr's heart attack.

"It was when we were leaving the doctor's office," she said. "Ted just . . . crumpled. I think he knew I was going to be all right, so he didn't have to hold up any longer. It was a lucky thing we were close to help."

Sophie and Liv exchanged quick glances. Their beloved Gran looked tired but strong. She was a small woman, with fine, thick gray hair pulled back from a face that had once been tanned but was paler after months spent indoors. She sat in her familiar chair beside a table set with photos of their granddad.

She picked one up and gazed at it.

"Your grandfather was sure looking forward to getting home," she said, stroking the picture frame. "How he hates the city." She put it back carefully. "But he'll be coming back to the Lucky Star, I just know it." She smiled around at them. "It's such a relief you'll all be here when he does."

Sophie glanced at her mother, perched bolt upright on the cowhide couch. So she hadn't told Gran they had to leave, and soon. No wonder Mom looked so stressed.

"Time for us to get to bed," Jess said, standing up and pointing a finger at Sophie and Liv. "Shane, with that bump on your head, you're staying right here on this couch. I don't want to hear any arguments. I'll get you some blankets and a pillow."

"Thank you, ma'am." Shane sighed. "I'm real sorry about your dad."

LIV'S PLAN

Back in their room upstairs, Liv sank onto her bed with a sigh. "To think that a few days ago I vowed I'd never sleep in this room again. Now Cactus Jack is better, Gran is home and I'm back here with you."

"Is that so bad?" Sophie asked.

Liv rolled over and looked at her twin. "No," she said slowly. "It's definitely better than sleeping in a stall." Sophie threw her pillow at Liv. Liv hurled it back.

"We'd better stop!" Sophie put a finger to her lips. "Shane's down there trying to sleep."

They were both silent, thinking about Shane and the last few amazing hours. "How much should we tell Mom?" Liv asked. "I mean, about the three coyotes, and the Heartbreak Hotel falling down around our ears?"

"As little as possible," warned Sophie. "She has enough to worry about with Granddad." She threw up her hands. "What's Mom going to do about her job now? Gran can't stay alone until he gets home. And they'll both need help on the ranch for a long time after that."

"Exactly!" Liv flopped back on her bed. "That's why we can't leave. We have to think of a way to stay here. You'll help me this time, won't you? You know what Mom said—two heads are better than one."

Sophie crossed the room and linked her index finger with Liv's. "Yes, I'll help." She hesitated. "It's not just because of Shane you want to stay, is it?"

"Shane?" Liv sat up. "Of course not. I love this ranch and the desert and I even love Rattlesnake Bend. But if there is one *person* I want to stay for, it's Brady. I've just started to get to know him. I can't leave."

"Brody Bolt? Are you *serious*?" Sophie leaned forward. "I thought you thought he was a hopeless goof."

"I changed my mind." Liv hugged her pillow. "I hope he comes back this weekend—we've got stuff to talk about."

"Someone just rode into the yard," Jess sang out from the kitchen, where she was fixing breakfast the next morning. "Can one of you see who it is?"

"It's Brady!" Liv hobbled to the front door, with Sophie close behind her.

Liv was wrong. When she opened the door, Liv saw Dayna Regis and her father, Sam, looking down at them from their golden palominos.

"Thought we'd ride over and see how you're doin' this fine Saturday mornin'." Sam took off his hat. "Hear you folks have a heap more trouble."

"That's nice of you, but it's kind of early." Liv stared straight at the chubby man on the gorgeous horse.

"We won't be stayin' long," Dayna said apologetically. Liv could see that although Dayna was as beautifully groomed and dressed as usual, there were dark circles under her eyes.

"You go get your ma and we can chat out here on the veranda," said Sam, climbing down off his horse. "Some coffee would go fine, if you have any."

"Dad!" Dayna said under her breath. She slid gracefully off Champagne and gathered the reins of both horses while her father stalked up on the veranda and plunked down in a wood chair under the skull of a cow nailed to a post.

"Used to have hundreds of cattle here on the Lucky Star," he blustered. "Now all that's left of them is these old skulls. Your grandparents are too old and sick to ranch."

"I'll get Mom," Liv said shortly.

"Like to talk to your grandmother, too." Sam banged his hat on his knee.

Dayna tied the reins of their horses around the veranda rail and followed Liv and Sophie inside.

"He's here about buying the ranch, isn't he?' Liv asked her.

Dayna nodded. "It's all he thinks about. When he heard that your granddad had had a heart attack, he couldn't wait. I'm sorry."

Liv went off to find her mother. Sophie stayed in the living room with Dayna. "Something else is wrong," she said hesitantly. "Want to talk about it?"

"Temo's gone." Dayna glanced at the floor and traced a tile with her boot. "He's gone to Mexico. I don't know when he'll be back."

She looked up at Sophie with tears in her eyes. "It wasn't just because of his cousin," she said. "I think his parents suspected how Temo and I felt about each other. They knew . . ." She glanced out at her father, now pacing the veranda. "They didn't want him to get in trouble with Dad."

"That's so unfair!" Sophie broke out. "But don't worry. Temo's crazy about you. He'll be back."

"Shh! Here comes your mom," Dayna warned.

Jess hurried past them through the door. They heard Sam speaking to her in his loud, blustering voice, then Jess's voice, low and urgent. "I don't want Mother to hear anything about selling the ranch right now," she said. "I'll call you in a day or two with our decision. Thank you for your offer."

She came back through the screen door and went straight to the kitchen without looking at Sophie or Dayna. They heard pots and pans being banged angrily on the stove.

Sam stuck his head in the door. "Might as well head out, daughter," he growled to Dayna. "Doesn't look like I'm going to get a cup of coffee here."

"I'd better go." Dayna grabbed Sophie's hand. "Sorry . . . about Dad . . . and there's something I wanted to tell Liv. Cheyenne got kicked off the Rattlesnake Riders team. She cut too many practices."

"I'll tell her," Sophie promised.

Dayna hurried away, wiping her eyes.

Sophie took a deep breath and headed for the kitchen, where her mom and Liv were nose to nose over the toaster.

"It's a good offer," Jess was saying, "and he's right. My parents are too old and sick to ranch."

"But *we're* not!" Liv reached for a piece of toast and buttered it carefully, right to the edges. "And Gran and Granddad's hearts would break if they had to leave the Lucky Star. You know it's true."

Jess put two more pieces of bread in the toaster, shoving the lever down angrily. "Of course it's true. But what are we going to do?"

Liv took her mother by the shoulders and steered her to a chair by the kitchen table. "It's simple, Mom. I'm fourteen, almost, but I can see it as clear as day. Why don't you quit your job—you love it here—you said so—" She rushed on, "Then you could rent out our house in Vancouver, or even sell it, which would give us enough money to live on and maybe find more water in Wild Horse Creek Canyon so we could raise cattle. Mark can come here to live with us. We can all look after Gran and Granddad and run the ranch."

Sophie gaped at her sister. *This* was Liv's plan? Sell the Vancouver house, live on the ranch, bring Mark here? Liv raised an eyebrow and Sophie remembered how she'd promised to support her idea. "It—it's brilliant, Mom," she stammered. "Trust Liv to come up with it."

"And the best part is," Liv went on, "we tell Dayna's miserable, interfering father to take a hike. We're not selling the Lucky Star."

"I shouldn't stoop to personal remarks," Jess said, "but that man is a toad! Imagine him showing up here this morning insisting I sell him the ranch!" She banged her fist on the table. "All right, I'll think about calling Mark."

"Don't tell him it's permanent," Liv suggested. "Say he's coming to the Lucky Star for a visit. Let us do the rest."

While they ate, Sophie passed on Dayna's news. "Poor Temo—and poor Dayna." Liv shook her head. "I hate to admit it, but I feel sorry for her."

"Dayna's not so bad when you get to know her," Sophie agreed. "I thought she was a real snob at first, but she can be nice. For instance, she had a message for you. There's still a spot on the Rattlesnake Riders. Cheyenne got kicked off."

"Yeehaw!" Liv shouted. "Another reason we have to stay. Now Cactus Jack just *has* to make a full recovery." She swept up her dishes, carried them to the sink and turned for the door. "I'd better go and check on him. Say hi to Mark and tell him he's going to be crazy about the ranch!"

Jess sighed. "Living with your sister is a bit like living in a tornado," she said, "but I think she might have a good idea about all of us moving here to the Lucky Star. What do you think?"

Sophie's face lit up. "The four of us would be together again, like a family," she said. "I'd love that." Mom was right, she thought, Liv could sweep you up in her whirlwind of ideas and enthusiasm, and sometimes you landed with a thump when she dashed off in another direction. But that was just Liv.

"So you might get to wear that fancy blue bridle after all," Liv explained to Cactus Jack in his stall. "All you have to do is get better so we can go to Rattlesnake Rider practices twice a week. Let me go get you some more water now."

"I like the way you talk to your horse," she heard a voice behind her say. Liv plunked down the water bucket and spun around. Brady was leaning on the stall door. He had snuck up without her noticing and she could feel herself flushing with surprise.

"Uh—hi!" she stammered. "I was just telling Cactus Jack that if he keeps getting better like this, we can get back to precision riding. Of course, the vet and Shane will have to give him the all clear . . ."

"Sure. That'll be good," Brady said, taking off his hat. "And speakin' of Shane, I've been wonderin'. I mean, I know when you told him yesterday we were going together, it was just an impulse. You're kind of impulsive, which I like, but we haven't talked about it, or anything . . ."

"Well, if you don't want to . . ." Liv's chin lifted.

"I didn't say that!" Brady's face turned red. He glanced away. "If I went with any girl, it would be you. But you seemed so stuck on Shane—I mean, you've never looked at me the way you look at him."

Liv took in his square face with its dark brows and unruly brown hair. She looked at his lanky body. He'd been so brave back at the Heartbreak Hotel. With his shoulders thrown back and one hand on the stall door, he didn't seem goofy or awkward.

"I'm looking at you that way now," she said softly, "in case you hadn't noticed."

Brady met her gaze. "Hey! You are!" he said joyfully. "Wow!" His eyes were bright as he swung open the stall door and marched forward, his arms spread wide.

As he reached for Liv, he stepped in the water bucket, tripped and flew into her with his arms flailing.

Cactus Jack, startled, jumped sideways. For a few seconds the stall was a scene of wild commotion, with Jack rearing and snorting.

"My stupid big feet!" Brady apologized when Liv had settled the horse down. "Are you . . . okay?"

"Don't worry," she said breathlessly, letting go of Jack's halter. "I shouldn't have left the water bucket there, where . . . a horse . . . could step in it." A helpless giggle wanted to burst from her lips, but she choked it back. She shouldn't laugh at Brady—not now!

Brady looked embarrassed. "How could you ever like somebody . . . who's always falling over you and dropping stuff?" he asked, rubbing his forehead. "Who's so darned clumsy?!"

"I'm not sure." Liv swallowed hard. "Do you think you might get over it someday?"

"Maybe." They both stopped talking and gazed into each other's eyes. Brady leaned gently forward once more. At that moment, Cactus Jack gave Liv's shoulder a hard nudge and she shot past Brady.

She collapsed on the straw, shaking with laughter. "Sorry. I think Jack's jealous. Horses don't always like to share."

Brady was laughing too as he helped her up. "I guess you're right. Maybe we can . . . talk sometime when we're not in his stall." His face grew serious. "Speakin' of horses, I have some news. The border police stopped by to tell my dad they escorted those three horse-smuggling coyotes out of the country. If they ever come back, they'll go to jail."

Liv sighed in relief. "I'm glad. That means Diego's safe and they won't be rounding up any more stallions for fights." She grabbed the empty water bucket and headed for the stall door.

As the water from the hose slowly filled the pail, Liv gazed out the barn door.

The desert, rosy brown in the morning light, beckoned. "I could saddle Trixie and we could go for a ride," she said to Brady. "Go up Wild Horse Creek Canyon. Talk about plans for the summer."

"The summer?" Brady's face clouded. "But you're leaving—"

Liv turned off the tap and hoisted the brimming pail. "Maybe not. In fact, I have an idea we'll stay right here on the Lucky Star Ranch for a long time." She took a deep, happy breath of sweet desert air. "Right where we belong."

GLOSSARY

bronc riding a rodeo event where the rider is on a horse that tries
  to buck or throw off the rider
burro donkey
diablo devil
hombre man
mesquite spiny, thicket-forming shrub or small tree with very hard,
  dense wood
muchacha female child

THE MYSTERY STALLION [1]

When thirteen-year-old twins Sophie and Liv spend their spring break on their grandparents' ranch in Arizona, they discover that the ranch in the Sonoran Desert is full of surprises. Both twins love horses, and they can't wait to meet their grandparents' herd of Spanish Barbs who roam freely on the three-thousand-acre ranch, but the girls soon encounter more than they bargained for.

When their grandfather's stallion is badly injured and the rest of the herd disappears, the twins—along with a good-looking cowhand named Shane—try to get to the bottom of the mystery.

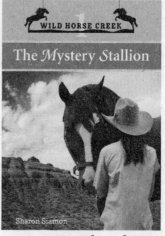

ISBN 978-1-55285-933-9

COYOTE CANYON [2]

When a precious colt goes missing on the Lucky Star Ranch, Liv and Sophie set out on a search—with the help of the young cowboy Shane. Will they find the foal before he is devoured by coyotes, cougars or other predators that prowl the desert canyons near Wild Horse Creek?

Other kids come to help, but Liv and Sophie don't know if they can trust them—at least not yet. And when the girls' search for the lost colt takes them deep into a maze of desert caves, Liv discovers a shocking secret.

ISBN 978-1-55285-934-6

MUSTANG MOUNTAIN SERIES

ISBN 978-1-55285-456-3

SKY HORSE [1]

Meg would do almost anything to get to Mustang Mountain Ranch, high in the Rocky Mountains. She wants a horse so badly. A sudden storm delays the trip and begins an adventure that takes Meg, her friend Alison and Alison's cousin Becky far off the beaten track. To reach Mustang Mountain, they'll need every scrap of courage they possess.

ISBN 978-1-55285-457-0

FIRE HORSE [2]

Meg, Alison and Becky are alone at the Mustang Mountain Ranch. When two horses go missing, the girls and their friend Henry set out on a rescue mission. Caught in a forest fire, they save themselves and the missing horses with the help of a wild mustang stallion.

NIGHT HORSE [3]

Returning to Mustang Mountain Ranch for the summer, Meg, Alison and Becky meet Windy, a beautiful mare about to give birth to her first foal. Meg learns a secret, too: a bounty hunter has been hired to kill the wild horses in the area. When Windy escapes the ranch, the girls move to protect the mare and the wild horses they love.

ISBN 978-1-55285-363-4

WILD HORSE [4]

On vacation at a ranch in Wyoming, Meg, Alison and Becky have a chance to ride wild horses. Alison doesn't care to participate. Her mood threatens the vacation. She changes, however, when she discovers a sick wild horse. As hope for the sick horse fades, Alison must conquer her anger and come up with a plan to save it.

ISBN 978-1-55285-413-6

RODEO HORSE [5]

Alison and Becky prepare to join the competitions at the Calgary Stampede. Becky wants to find out more about Rob, the mysterious brother of a champion barrel racer. Meg, meanwhile, is stuck in New York, longing to join the Stampede. An accident threatens the girls' plans. Or was it an accident?

ISBN 978-1-55285-467-9

BRAVE HORSE [6]

A phantom horse, a missing friend, a dangerous valley filled with abandoned mine shafts . . . not exactly what Meg, Alison and Becky were expecting on vacation at the Mustang Mountain Ranch. Becky had expected a peaceful time without her annoying cousin Alison. Alison had expected to be traveling in Paris. And Meg had planned to meet with Thomas. Instead, the girls must organize a rescue. Will they be in time?

ISBN 978-1-55285-528-7

FREE HORSE [7]

A new adventure begins while Meg and Thomas care for a neighboring lodge and its owner's rambunctious ten-year-old stepson, Tyler. The trouble starts when Tyler opens a gate and lets the ranch horses out. In his search for the missing horses, Thomas discovers that someone is catching and selling wild horses. Could it be Tyler's brother Brett and his friends? A hailstorm hits and Thomas fails to return to the lodge. Can Meg and Tyler find Thomas and save the wild horses?

ISBN 978-1-55285-608-6

SWIFT HORSE [8]

Alison Chant is angry at the world. She wants a new horse, but everything gets in her way. First, her mom says, "No more horses!" Then, she finds the horse of her dreams, but it belongs to a young girl named Kristy Jones, who refuses to sell her beloved Skipper. Finally, Alison takes matters into her own hands, only to get Skipper and herself into terrible trouble at a barrel race. Who can save her? Does she have the courage and strength to make things right?

ISBN 978-1-55285-659-8

ISBN 978-1-55285-720-5

DARK HORSE [9]

Becky Sanderson has entered her first endurance challenge. She and her mother's chestnut mare, Windy, have to race fifty grueling miles over rough mountain trails. Becky is confident she can do it, especially with the help of her friend Rob. But Rob unexpectedly gets distracted by another racer, a willowy blonde whose behavior is more than a little suspicious. Will Becky's jealousy get in the way of her finishing the race? Becky finds herself caught up in a vicious race with riders who will stop at nothing to win.

ISBN 978-1-55285-798-4

STONE HORSE [10]

The future of the Mustang Mountain Ranch is in jeopardy: the government wants to close the ranch. Starting a horse camp for kids might be the only way to save it.

Inspired by the legend of a jade rock hidden in the cave of the stone horse, Meg and a group of uncooperative campers set out for the peak of Mustang Mountain.

Can Meg and her friends survive the mountain, win the girls over and make the camp a success? The future of Mustang Mountain Ranch depends on it.

SADDLE ISLAND SERIES

GALLOP TO THE SEA [1]

Set on Nova Scotia's wild and windswept eastern shore, *Gallop to the Sea*, the first installment in this series, introduces the spirited Kelsie MacKay as she tries to rescue a rebellious horse named Caspar. Kelsie plans to swim Caspar to a mysterious deserted island before his owner ships him off for auction.

A violent storm develops, putting Kelsie and Caspar in great danger. Will they make it to shore safely? This first adventure from Saddle Island puts readers in the thick of intrigue and adventure.

ISBN 978-1-55285-713-7

SECRETS IN THE SAND [2]

In *Secrets in the Sand*, Kelsie MacKay has a problem. She has a chance to add three more horses to her Saddle Island refuge, but there's no money to keep them. Kelsie's counting on a rich stranger from Boston. Her brother Andy is banking on finding treasure on Saddle Island to get them out of their money fix.

But Saddle Island doesn't give up its secrets easily. Wild winds, tides and dangerous rocks threaten Kelsie, Andy and their friend Jen. Can they escape, and will Kelsie and Andy find a way to keep the horses and stay in Dark Cove?

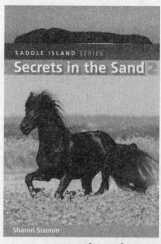

ISBN 978-1-55285-714-4

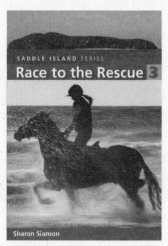

ISBN 978-1-55285-855-4

RACE TO THE RESCUE [3]

In this final book of the Saddle Island trilogy, set on Nova Scotia's wild and windswept eastern shore, a strange man mysteriously appears on the island. Could he have anything to do with the arrival of a thoroughbred named Diamond?

In *Race to the Rescue*, Kelsie MacKay is startled by a sudden request to rescue a racehorse. She has to make a snap decision. And when she agrees to take Diamond she sets off a chain of events that will change Saddle Island forever. Fires, smugglers and shipwrecks challenge Kelsie, her brother Andy and their friend Jen to the utmost. Can they save Diamond and the other horses from disaster?

ABOUT THE AUTHOR

Author Sharon Siamon was born in the province of Saskatchewan in Canada's west. As a teenager, she fell in love with the desert of the American Southwest. Riding a horse across the wide open spaces toward distant mountains was a memory she never forgot. Although she has lived most of her life in the east, the West keeps drawing her back. When she heard the story of Spanish colonial horses, bred for generations on family ranches in Arizona and New Mexico, she knew she wanted to write about these amazing "iron horses."

Sharon lives in the country near Perth, Ontario, with her husband, Jeff, and dog, Brio.

Visit Sharon's updated website at www.sharonsiamon.com
or email her at sharon@sharonsiamon.com.